DEAD CALM

ARCANE SOULS WORLD

GRAVE TALKER SERIES BOOK THREE

ANNIE ANDERSON

DEAD CALM

ARCANE SOULS WORLD

Grave Talker Book 3

International Bestselling Author
Annie Anderson

Edited by Angela Sanders
Cover Design by Tattered Quill Designs

www.annieande.com

For S.
You know why.
Here's to 15 more.

Daughter of Souls & Silence

Lady of Madness & Moonlight

Sister of Embers & Echoes

Priestess of Storms & Stone

Queen of Fate & Fire

PHOENIX RISING SERIES

(Formerly the Ashes to Ashes Series)

Flame Kissed

Death Kissed

Fate Kissed

Shade Kissed

Sight Kissed

ROMANTIC SUSPENSE NOVELS

SHELTER ME SERIES

Seeking Sanctuary

Reaching Refuge

"Go all the way with it. Do not back off. For once, go all the goddamn way with what matters."

— ERNEST HEMINGWAY

I needed a vacation.

That was the headline that blasted across my thoughts as I stared at the note that had been so carefully placed on my counter. I was supposed to be going on a teensy getaway with Bishop. After the bullshit we'd gone through over the last few days, taking some time off had seemed paramount. Taking a brief pause from my contemplation, I found my shirt and yanked it back on before continuing my internal deliberation.

As I stared at the cardstock, the devil on my shoulder was making a solid case for ignoring literally everything in my life, packing a bag, and hightailing it to some undiscovered corner of the map with no cell service which could only be accessed by boat. At this point, I was considering moving into a yurt or something just to not have to deal with the utter shitshow that had become my life.

Angel Darby began arguing in favor of staying to find my psychopath of a brother, while Devil Darby was still painting pictures of Bishop and me wearing very little clothing in a hut on the beach, sipping Mai Tais. I had to admit, Devil Darby was winning that fight, hands-down. And what did the line "Your mother can't protect you anymore" mean?

As far as I knew—and that wasn't much when it came to Mariana, but still—she hadn't done a damn thing to protect me a day in her life. This damn note was a taunt—a dare. And I didn't like it one bit.

Without much thought on my part, I yanked a paper towel from the holder and picked up the note to inspect it. There wasn't a damn clue to be had on the thing, at least not to my naked eye.

You know that means you could just pretend you never saw it, right? Just drop it like a hot potato and scamper off to a cabin in the woods with Bishop.

See? Devil Darby had a solid plan.

And what happens when X doesn't just stop at notes? Then it's Texas Chainsaw Massacre *time with a side of* Halloween *for dessert.*

And there was Angel Darby coming in for the buzzkill.

I was still mired in my internal debate until the note was yanked from my hands. Slowly turning to the culprit, I silently blinked out my shock. Azrael stood bold as brass in my living room, an expression of unmitigated rage on his face. And while the rage wasn't anything to sneeze at, that was not what had shocked me. Don't get me wrong, my Angel of Death father just popping up in my living room was definitely shock-worthy. However, it was the set of ebony wings protruding from his back that really got my attention.

"I swear to everything holy, it's like you're trying to get killed," he growled, incredibly put out for some reason.

Well, it's not like I called him here.

"Is there a particular reason you're in my living room looking like the Grim Reaper, or is this just part of your charm?"

His form flickered a little, his hair turning white as a faint purple-tinted his irises before they—along with his wings—winked out of sight. "I'm in your living room on the off chance your brother has decided to put a blood curse on this note," Azrael said, waving the cardstock in my face. "Honestly, out of everyone, I sort of figured I wouldn't have to worry too much about you, but the last few days have proved me wrong on that front ten-fold."

That was totally not fair. "No part of this has been my fault. Not the poltergeist, not the ABI building attack, and certainly not the Dubois nest debacle. And if I remember right, wasn't it you who sent me there in the first damn place? No, sir. If anyone is to blame, it's you and your bullshit lack of information."

Was I yelling at a death deity? Why, yes. Yes, I was.

"Picking up a note, Darby? Really?"

Why that victim-blaming son of a bitch…

He flinched at my internal tone, but I didn't let him off the hook with just that one. "This isn't a crime scene, Azrael, and I don't see a dead body anywhere. I should be allowed to touch things in my own house."

And while I'd cursed myself right as I'd touched the damn thing, I didn't need his bullshit chastisement.

"Yes, and you shouldn't have to worry about your siblings killing you either, but here we are. Haven't you figured out by now that X has every intention of killing you?"

Why no, I hadn't quite figured that out yet, Azrael. Thanks for the head's up.

"Haven't you figured out that that particular qualifier doesn't make him special? I'm a cop, a woman, and I have a penchant for sticking my nose in other people's affairs. X isn't the first, nor will he be the last person to try. What I want to know is why you think he'd curse me, and moreover, I want to know what it is you're hiding. There's no way you'd just pop in here on a whim."

I was about to spew a sight bit more profanities at my absentee birth father when my doorbell rang. Grumbling, I spun to answer it. On my front stoop was a blissfully tall man in a tight black T-shirt and a pair of jeans that had to be against a decency code of some kind.

Still, I was so mad, the whole of Bishop La Roux barely registered.

"Please tell me you have tacos," I blurted, the hope in my voice a very real thing.

I needed those tacos. Bad.

Bishop revealed a white bag from behind his back, a frown marring his face. Then his gaze strayed from me to the man standing smack-dab in the middle of my living room. "We aren't going on vacation, are we?"

No, I was pretty sure we were not.

After setting aside three of the twelve tacos in the bag for Bishop—*what? I'm not a monster*—I got busy munching while I gave my father the stink-eye. I did this for two reasons.

One: Azrael was rather put out that I was pausing our family squabble to eat my food and was acting like a big baby about it. Two: I still wasn't quite over the fact that he was being far too cagey for a man who professed a desire to keep me breathing.

He knew a hell of a lot more than he was saying, and it was pissing me off.

Bishop and Azrael eyed each other as they sat at opposite ends of my couch, both of them smart enough not to sit in my favorite chair. Neither of them spoke, so the silence was only broken by my rather loud crunching as I unabashedly wolfed down my tacos.

"Well, isn't this a sad sight," an Irish voice remarked, and I paused in my oppressive crunching to glare at the man.

Hildenbrand O'Shea—AKA, my wayward and totally dead grandfather, Hildy—hovered over one of my barstools. Well, I supposed he was sitting, but I didn't really understand the mechanics of the act. Could ghosts really sit on furniture, or did their spectral butts just hover over it? It was a question for the ages and one I hadn't ever thought to ask.

Out of the three living-ish people in the room, only two of us could actually see or hear Hildy—a benefit of being whole or part death deity, I supposed—but only I acknowledged the ghost.

"What's sad, Hildy? The fact that I'm still in my living room, even though I'm supposed to be on vacation, or that my birth father is a raging asshole?"

Both Azrael and Bishop started at my words, even though neither should be surprised that I'd talk to a ghost right in front of them. I'd been hiding my whole life, and I wasn't too keen on that being the status quo.

"I'm not an asshole," Azrael muttered, his expression almost a full-on pout.

My chuckle was mirthless as I answered, "What would you call a man that never gave you a straight answer, spoke in only vague pronouncements, and refused to give even a little insight to a rather nasty dilemma that could potentially kill you? Because that sounds like an asshole to me."

"I thought you were leaving, lass. Why are you not?" Leave it to Hildy to get me back on track. I had a feeling there would only be so many times that I could get away with calling Azrael the asshole he most definitely was before there would be consequences.

Jutting out my chin, I gestured to the note my stupid, murdering brother left for me as I fought off a shudder. He was in my house. X had been in my. Fucking. House.

I was having a tough time not hosing everything

down in bleach or setting it on fire. That teensy bit of knowledge made my skin crawl... though it still wasn't enough to put me off my food.

Hildy's normally genial face turned to stone as he read the note.

"What the fuck is this supposed to mean? Do you think he's done something to...?" He swallowed, his form flickering to solid and back to transparent in a blink.

"I don't know," I murmured, studying Hildy with dawning realization.

As much as he professed his disappointment in my mother, she was still his kid. No one wanted to think about losing a child—which had to be tough when said child was a card-carrying menace to the planet as a whole. I took another bite of the taco as I shifted to study Azrael, who met my gaze with a nod.

I guess now I was getting it. Still...

Hildy himself turned to my father. "Is she alive? Just tell me if—"

"You know I can't tell you that. I can tell you that she hasn't made it to me, but you and I both know that doesn't mean anything."

And there went that other shoe again. I'd been so preoccupied with X being in my house that I hadn't really given much thought to what might have been done to Mariana. She could be more than just captured, more than just dead. What if X absorbed souls like I could? What if he tortured them?

What if he did something worse?

I wasn't such a monster that the thought of Mariana biting it didn't sting. Nor was I such a heartless cow that the idea of her being tortured was a happy thought. That didn't mean I'd be rushing out to save her ass, though.

Hildy shook his head at my father, a bit of rage making his whole body solid. "You're the only person playing by the rules, Azrael. Your boy isn't, and neither is my daughter. Stop hiding what you know or leave us be. You're doing us no favors by keeping secrets."

Azrael stood; the measured pace of his rise from the couch made the tiny hairs on my arms stand on end. His hair flickered from black to white, and coupling that with the eerie purple glow to his eyes, my foot took an involuntary step back.

"I am the only one playing by the rules, because if I don't, people die. If I don't, reality as we know it ceases to be. I play by the fucking rules because I damn well have to, and I will not be chided by a child without the barest inkling of what the universe is."

"Then why are you here?" That question came from Bishop, who was still sitting calm as you please on my couch. His face was a mask of stone, and I couldn't get even a glimmer of his emotions. He simply stared at the Angel of Death like he was missing a tee time or something. "You can't tell her what she needs to know, and you can't bend the rules, and you refuse to even let us buy a damn vowel in this shit. You're here for a reason, right? So, enlighten us. Otherwise, stop just showing up when it suits you. Darby already has a parent who does that."

The bite of taco in my mouth turned to sawdust, and I struggled to swallow it. I definitely should have listened to Devil Darby and just grabbed his hand and let him whisk me off to some far away locale. This whole tableau was getting us nowhere, and I didn't need the added reminder that I got the short end of the stick in the parenting department.

Fixing my gaze to my counter, I tried not to let Bishop's pronouncement sting, but it did little good.

"Your brother attempted to kill another of your siblings a few months ago while you were in prison. He did it with a blood curse administered via a note on her bed. It didn't work, but your sister is different from you in many ways. You would not have been as lucky. Your distress at the note called to me, so I came. When I saw the note, I thought..." Azrael trailed off and shook his head, his hair falling back to black with the motion. "He seems determined to kill you both, and the more that his plans fail, the more desperate he becomes."

I wanted to be shitty and say something along the lines of "Tell me something I don't know," but the reality of it all was staring me in the face. X wanted me dead, and he was getting desperate.

And no one wanted a desperate murderer after them.

Especially me.

2

While I knew Azrael was still keeping secrets, it seemed harder and harder to blame the man. Despite my inherent nature to ask questions, I refrained.

Barely.

"Thank you for looking out for me," I murmured, staring at my half-eaten taco. "If there is something you can tell us, that would be appreciated, but I get it now." All of this was bigger than my questions. It was bigger than me—than all of us.

I wanted to know who my sister was. I wanted to know if she was okay—if I could meet her. A teensy corner of my brain was screaming to know if my awful mother was alive. But what I wanted would have to take a back seat.

"What do you want me to do? Stay here and let him come for me? Attack? Go into hiding? What?" Two of the three were palatable enough that I wouldn't puke on my shoes, but I doubted that was what he'd pick.

Azrael stared at his shoes in silence as he ripped a hand through his long hair. "Don't you think I would tell you if I knew? Your brother has kept himself from me for so long, I can't predict what he'll do. I don't know what will be safer. I don't know how he keeps finding you both."

Dread yawned wide at his words—not for me, though. No, my dread was directed at the man who just unlocked a piece of the puzzle. *Your brother has kept himself from me for so long…*

Kept himself from me.

Meaning Azrael knew who he was, knew what he looked like. Knew what he was capable of. And still, he'd said nothing.

At the direction of my thoughts, Azrael lifted his head and met my gaze. His irises flashed purple before they flickered back to black. That was a guilty tell if I ever saw one.

"You knew him before he started this mess," I accused aloud and felt the air of the whole room shift. I felt more than saw Bishop shifting in his seat as Hildy drew closer to me. "You know who he is. What he looks like. You've known this whole time. He isn't a mystery to you. Just to me. The woman he's trying to kill."

Azrael flinched, a flash of guilt flitting across his face before he shut it down. That's when I knew he wasn't going to tell me what I needed to know, nor was he going to admit to a damn thing.

Pretty standard, really.

"And what was the catalyst for him hiding from you?" I asked, connecting the dots in my head. "What happened before he started killing your other children?"

At the shame stamped all over him, I knew my gut was right.

"What did you do to him, Azrael? Because no one goes on a murdering spree unprompted unless they're a sociopath. And people don't protect sociopaths." At least in *my* experience they didn't. And usually, people needed a motive to do horrendous things. The power of Azrael's throne used to seem like a big enough incentive but not anymore. "Tell me—are you protecting a sociopath, or does my brother have a good reason for killing your kids?"

All the potential motives swirled in my head, but I wasn't prepared for the one he gave.

"I did nothing."

Snorting, I shook my head. "This seems like a *lot* of

vengeance for a little bit of 'nothing.' Got to say, I'm not buying it."

Azrael's form flashed again, only this time his wings came out to play, the dark mass of them spreading wide enough to knock a lamp from an end table. I couldn't spare a glance at the crash of glass on my floor. I was too focused on the glowing violet eyes that seemed to bore into my very soul.

"No, child. My sin is that I did nothing. Had I broken my rules then, we wouldn't be in this mess now." And then as if he had never been there at all, he disappeared.

"Well, that told us dick," Bishop muttered as he approached the island, swiping a taco from his stack. He hastily unwrapped the morsel and popped an end in his mouth. When his eyes went wide, I started giggling, and as they rolled back into his head at the sheer awesomeness, a much-needed laugh burst from my lips. He swallowed and went in for another bite, and then the thing was gone.

"You let me sit there and not even taste these bits of heaven this whole time?" Bishop accused, unwrapping his second taco, a scowl playing at the corners of his mouth.

"You're the one who walked in there and bought them. How was I supposed to know you didn't snag some for yourself?"

Bishop chuckled. "I'm not messing with a bruja unless I have to, Darby. Especially not that one. The only reason she sold to me at all was because I told her they were for you. No way was I going to steal one. That woman probably put a curse on the bag."

I simply shrugged. It didn't take a rocket scientist to figure out that the Bernal's were of the arcane world. I mean, how else would they be getting customers way out there in the sticks? No signage or advertising in this day and age? Of course there had to be magic involved.

The Bernal's being arcane made sense. Too bad my father's vague-as-shit "nothing" comment did not.

"I swear, if I could, I'd shake that man," Hildy griped, still staring at the spot where Azrael stood just minutes before.

"Get in line," I muttered and popped the rest of my unfinished taco in my mouth.

The sound of my back door opening sent a spike of dread through me until my partner, J, emerged from the back hall. Jeremiah Cooper had been my friend since before I could remember and had used that entrance all of five times since I'd owned this house. Each time, his tidings hadn't exactly been pleasant. Add in the fact that he was supposed to be on a first date with the hunkiest of hunks, and I had a feeling this would be no exception.

Plus, J had his "cop face" on. The same one he used

when he told families their loved one died. I didn't like that face, didn't like the crinkled brow over his ice-blue eyes or the frown set to his mouth. That expression had me gripping the counter like a lifeline. I couldn't even ask what was wrong.

All I could do was hold on and wait.

J sighed like he was gearing himself up, and the suspense was going to give me a fucking ulcer.

"Killian is going to walk through that door in about five minutes, and I need you not to freak out," he began, and a wave of relief hit me so hard, I practically fell on my ass. I cared about approximately ten people in this world and three of them were in this kitchen. I wobbled so hard, Bishop skirted the island to hold me up.

"As an FYI, I'm going to need you to make sure you preface every instance of the use of that face by telling me my dad is alive, mm-kay?"

J rolled his eyes. "Why do you think I said his name first? I'm not an idiot. But that's not the point. Killian is about to drop a bomb on you, and I need you *not* to freak."

"When in the history of ever have I freaked?"

All three men—both living *and* dead—stared at me like I just told the mother of all whoppers.

Okay, so I'm an excitable kind of girl. Sue me.

"Whatever. Spill it." It had to be big for him to miss

his date with Jimmy. And I'd much rather think about whatever the hell was up with him than the murderous brother with an ax to grind. Though I had a feeling whatever he was about to say would be related.

"There was a body found in Dove Creek Cemetery."

At the name of the cemetery, I was sorely tempted to yank the bottle of vodka from my freezer and start guzzling. When I was nine, I'd thought the name was beautiful as I read the etched plaque on the stone wall surrounding the graveyard. I'd thought if my mother had to be buried anywhere, I was glad it was a pretty place with a pretty name.

"A female body was discovered about thirty minutes ago. Normally, that would be bad enough, but..."

I started nodding, wanting him to get it all out before I made my decision to start mainlining booze.

Your mother can't help you anymore. That's what the note said, right?

"They found her on top of your mother's grave."

Theeeeere it was.

My gut bottomed out as inexplicable tears hit my eyes. It didn't make any sense, and yet, it so did. Even though she was a bitch on wheels, even though she was the fucking worst, the thought of Mariana not being in this world anymore still hurt something awful.

I swallowed hard, trying to get the tears out of my throat. "Is it her?"

J seemed to brace himself. "I don't know. The description of the body matches, but I haven't been to the scene."

My gaze broke from J's as I met Hildy's eyes. A million thoughts seemed to pass between us in an instant, and I knew he was experiencing the same conflicted grief I was. The same senseless tears that fell down my cheeks raced down his as well. What a pair we made—the last two vestiges of this dreadful woman's family, crying over someone who would have never mourned us in turn.

We were idiots.

Dashing at the stupid tears on my cheeks, I pivoted on a heel and made my way to my bedroom. Until I saw it for myself, whoever was on that grave was not my mother. They just weren't.

Busying my hands, I put on my gear—blessed rosaries, vest, and all the other accoutrement that went with me to every crime scene. If I were lucky, no one would stop me from sticking my nose in this mess. Everyone in town was under the assumption that Mariana Adler was already dead, so it was totally possible that the connection hadn't been made.

Then again, I seriously doubted my luck would *ever* be that good.

By the time I emerged from my room, my father had arrived. I met his gaze as I slid my service weapon into its spin holster. Killian Adler might not have been my real dad, but that didn't stop me from resembling the man. Tall and blond, his blue eyes were just a shade lighter than mine and held just the same weight.

"Ready to go?" I asked, breaking the tense silence that seemed to have settled over my entire house.

My dad shook his head at me, holding out a hand like he wanted a hug. Normally, I'd be the first person to give him one, but right then, I just couldn't. I didn't want a hug or a pat on the back or some other such platitude. I'd had all that as a kid when I'd thought my mother was dead. I'd hated it then, and I sure as shit would hate it now.

My father's frown deepened when I didn't take the offered hug. "They aren't going to let you take point on this, Darby."

I ignored that pronouncement and locked eyes with Bishop. "You show him the note?"

Bishop's face was a blank mask, but still, he answered me with a clipped, "Yep."

"You have any objections to me going?" I couldn't say why I asked that question, but I did. I was pretty sure if he answered in the affirmative, I'd be going anyway, but his support would be nice.

Bishop's half-smile was exasperated and sexy as hell. "Nope. Though, I doubt you'd listen if I had any."

My lips curved into an unrepentant grin, which felt odd given the situation. I directed my attention back to my dad. "How about we see what Cap says and go from there? Shall we?"

In hindsight, I most definitely should have taken his advice.

3

I hadn't been to Dove Creek Cemetery in over a decade, but that didn't stop me from remembering everything about the place. Little had changed over the years, blending seamlessly with the memory of the last time I'd visited. It still had the tall stone edifice with the impossibly high wrought-iron gate. Walled cemeteries were a rarity in Tennessee, and it always creeped me out that the ones here were there in the first place. Adding that the damn things were eight feet tall, and I'd had always been a little afraid of what they might be keeping in here.

Man, if my nine-year-old self could see me now...

I'd stopped coming to visit my mother's grave around about the time that ghosts became a solid part of my daily life. Graveyards weren't my favorite places to be once I got an up-close-and-personal peek at the afterlife. Really, who could blame me? The only ghost I'd wanted to talk to wasn't anywhere to be found.

A swarm of black-and-whites were parked at the gates, their lights flashing like beacons even in the bright daylight. It was like they were trying to gather looky-loos. The general public of Haunted Peak had a penchant for minding their own business, true, but a bunch of cop cars barring the way to an already-creepy cemetery? A small crowd gathered at the entrance trying to get a glimpse of the to-do.

Luckily, someone had the forethought to tape off the gate, even if they had Jefferson in charge of crowd control. That was like installing a fancy alarm system only to leave your door unlocked, but no one asked for my opinion.

A crotchety-looking woman with peach pin curls waved her cane at the young officer as he bobbed and weaved to miss it. Sporting an honest-to-god muumuu and house slippers, it was all I could do not to start giggling as she attempted to bean the rookie in the head. "I want to know why there are po-lice cars lined up on the street every other day. This is a nice town with good people. You start talking, young man, right now."

Jefferson managed to catch the offending piece of

aluminum before it beaned him on the head. "Ma'am, I'm going to need you to stop that this instant."

I stifled a snicker as I threaded through the crowd, Bishop and J following close behind me as my father brought up the rear. My ghostly grandfather had likely already flowed through the crowd to assess the scene, but I would have loved to have seen his reaction to the ruckus.

Most of the onlookers parted once they saw me, my pariah status incredibly effective when it came to skipping ahead of the crowd, but it was J who got the rest moving.

"Ladies and gentlemen, I'm going to have to ask you to disperse. This is an official crime scene, and you are impeding the access of officers of the law." Several crowd members buzzed with outrage, but J's good old boy reputation had plenty of them moving on. "Go on now."

Just about everyone started breaking off, except the formidable elderly woman with her cane still in Jefferson's hand. She met my gaze with her steely one, and I found myself apprehensive of a woman who could probably be blown over by a stiff wind.

"Jefferson, give the nice lady her cane back, will you?" I suggested, and the rookie stared at the cane in his hand like he had no idea how it got there.

"He-here, ma'am," he stuttered, passing it back to

her like one would offer a steak to a grizzly bear. She snatched it from his grip but wobbled slightly, which had me reaching for her arm to steady her.

The woman's eyes narrowed further, and if she did that anymore, I doubted she'd be able to see.

"I didn't need your help," she hissed, seemingly affronted at my assistance.

"Sure you didn't," I muttered, narrowing my eyes right back before addressing my least favorite rookie. "Jefferson, why don't you escort this nice young lady home?" I may have put a little of a command into my tone because Jefferson snapped to.

"A-absolutely, Detective Adler." He threaded an arm around the woman's elbow and gently guided her away. "Come on, Mrs. Lindell, I'll take you home." Seemingly thwarted, the old battle-ax tottered off with Jefferson, griping the whole way.

"You know that lady is a crone, right?" Bishop whispered in my ear, making me jump.

I whipped my head to look at him, my eyes narrowing in affront. "That's rude. Just because she's an old lady—"

"No," he muttered, shaking his head. "Like an arcane crone. Usually, they work in folk medicine and spin stories, but quite a few have enough juice to cause a problem. I thought this town was supposed to be mostly humans?"

My mental Rolodex flipped through all the arcane cases that had landed in my lap over the years. I couldn't say whether or not the majority of the population was human or arcane, but my caseload definitely favored the latter.

The best I could do was shrug. "I bet Jimmy could tell us. But I thought arcaners had to register or something?"

I was legitimately stalling now. When I'd heard the news, I'd been all about finding out the truth, but being here? I didn't know if I was ready to be slapped in the face with it just yet.

"They do," he agreed, stepping closer to me to bump my shoulder with his. "You ready to go in there, or do you need a few?"

Tears pricked at my eyes, and I had to force myself to swallow them down. Mariana hadn't been my mother in an exceedingly long time. It didn't make a single bit of sense for me to be this emotional about the situation. Too bad my tear ducts hadn't got the message.

"I'm good," I lied, shoving all my stupid, senseless emotions down. I could do this. Probably. Ducking under the yellow police tape, I marched through the gates of the cemetery as I scanned the headstones.

Dove Creek was a relatively large cemetery with mausoleums and crypts, as well as fenced-off family plots. Large trees dotted the hills with well-maintained stone benches. It was a far cry from the historical graveyard at the center of town, which likely had to do with its occupants. Many of the wealthiest families in town had entire sections to themselves, their ghosts milling about as they mingled with the living.

I hadn't known it on my first visit, but this cemetery was typically bursting with specters.

My mother's grave was close to the center of the cemetery, with several people standing around a taped-off square, doing nothing much at all. I was about to head that way when a hand grabbed mine. It was a familiar hand, the warmth of my father's fingers cradling mine, sending me right back to the first time we'd come here together. A wave of grief caught me for a solid second, and it was all I could do not to start bawling.

The story had been that Mariana had died in a car accident—a revered wife and mother gone too soon from this world. I figured it had been an easy lie for my father to tell, way easier to tell a pretty falsehood rather than the ugly truth. I couldn't say I wouldn't have done the same in his shoes, knowing what I did now, though a part of me wished I would have known how little my mother cared for me then.

Maybe if I'd known, I wouldn't have wasted all those years looking for her ghost. Truth be told, I wasn't too keen on finding it now.

I squeezed my father's hand before letting it go, pointing my feet in the direction of the crowd. By the time I made it up the hill, I was sweating, the late spring Tennessee sun scorching my mood to a solid eleven on my bitch-o-meter.

The first person I came across was Sal Whitestone, the detective smartly on the proper side of the police tape. His eyes grew round at my approach, and he nudged the man to his left before his gaze skittered away. At Sal's nudging, my captain's head flew up from his inspection of the tablet in his hands. Surprise colored his features before a resigned sort of indignation settled there. His gaze left me and went to my father.

"Killian, I thought I—"

My father raised his hand for him to stop. "I did, and she didn't listen. You're her boss—you tell her."

Cap ground his teeth as he rolled his eyes at my dad, slipping an arm around my shoulders and leading me away from the crowd. "You know good and well that you can't be here in any official capacity, right?"

I slipped my badge off my belt and handed it to him. "I don't know what you're talking about," I said airily. "I'm not here at all. I'm certainly not here to make sure things are done to regs with exactly zero fuck-ups." My gaze trailed past him and landed on a man with no booties in the middle of the scene, standing over the deceased. "Well, *almost* no fuck-ups."

Cap turned, his gaze following mine until it, too, landed on the idiot in the middle of the taped-off square. He sighed as he pinched his brow, shaking his head. "Exactly. You aren't here. You certainly aren't ripping that idiot a new one for contaminating the scene or making his life a living hell until he extricates his head from his ass. I saw nothing."

I fought off a smile, trying not to snicker.

"But I am holding onto this for a little bit. Got your service weapon?" I nodded, unclipping the holster from my belt and handing it over. He slipped my badge in his pocket as he held onto the holstered Glock. "You're still covered, right?"

I gave him a sly smile. "Of course."

Cap nodded. "Good. I'll be taking your father with me. I know it can't be her, but it sure as hell looks like it. He doesn't need to see that."

Cap—AKA, Uncle Dave—had been my father's best friend since they were in diapers. He'd known me since *I* was in diapers, too. "Take care of him, will you? This is..." I trailed off, letting my gaze drift over everything. "This is a lot."

"It's a lot for you, too, kid." He said it gently, even though he likely knew it would earn him a frown. "Yeah, yeah. Emotions are for the weak," he muttered, pulling me into a quick squeeze. "Give the new medical examiner hell, will you?"

I pushed back to look Cap in the eye.

"That douche canoe is the new ME?" I hissed under my breath, affronted on every level. Who in the high holy hell had thought that was a good idea? The poor guy didn't look old enough to vote, let alone do the job he was solidly fucking up just at a glance.

Cap inclined his head before giving me a gentle slug to the shoulder. "Do me proud."

I expected the smile on my face could rival *The Grinch* in evilness.

"That's my girl. Let Cooper know he's lead, will you?"

Nodding in answer, I took off in the direction of the crowd, it, too, parting like the one outside the cemetery but for a vastly different reason. As the reigning queen of pranking on staff at the Haunted Peak Police Department, I was feared on every level, but no more so than when it came to fucking up crime scenes. Usually, I was a live and let live kind of gal, but all it took to make me a raging bitch from the depths of Satan's anus was to jack with one of my scenes.

Sal took one look at me and sent a pitying glance at the poor shmuck kneeling over the deceased. I thought I heard a muttered "Good luck" before he shook his head. I gave him a wink, and the aging detective shot me a smile, likely happy as hell it wasn't him on the receiving end of my wrath this time.

I let my gaze fall to the body, zeroing in on the woman's face that was pulled into the waxy mask of death. My gut pitched as I studied her features, my mind trying desperately to make them anything but what they appeared to be.

X's note was correct.

My mother most definitely would not be able to help me anymore.

4

I prayed my face revealed nothing of the bitter grief and fear swirling in my middle as I got myself together. I had to focus on something—anything —else besides the fact that my mother was splayed out like an offering on top of her unused grave. Settling on ripping the new ME a new one, I slipped crime scene booties on my feet and gloved up, the whole time glaring at the small man royally screwing up my scene.

Okay, so it was J's scene, but I knew for a fact he didn't care about fuck all except putting murderers in jail, so I didn't feel too badly about mentally claiming it.

The freshly cut grass was a mess of blood spatter and viscera, the torso of Mariana's body damn near hollowed out. I swallowed bile, ignoring everyone and everything but the man squatting over my mother's corpse, his feet firmly planted in the blood-soaked dirt.

"Detective Adler," J called from behind me, "Please meet our new medical examiner, Dr. Yates."

At the sound of his name, the ME's head popped up, and I realized I'd been too generous with his age. Dr. Yates didn't even look old enough to shave. With sandy-blond hair and a decent jaw, I had a feeling he would eventually grow into his features sometime in the next decade.

The new ME's expression settled into a frown before seeming to dismiss both J and I as he returned to examining the body. What he thought he was going to do, I had no idea. Even from fifteen feet away, I could tell my mother's body did not hold a liver, so getting time of death via liver temp was out. His only other job on the scene was to determine a preliminary cause of death, and that didn't take a rocket scientist to figure out.

This was a murder, a gruesome one to boot.

"Tell me, Dr. Yates, perchance did you complete your forensic pathology residency?" I called, doing my very best not to alert the young doctor that he was already on my bad side as I crossed the tape.

"Of course I have," he replied, exasperation coloring

each word like slime as he continued his examination without so much as a glance in my direction.

I minced my way through the scene, careful of my foot placement as I moved closer. "Super. Then can you explain to me why you are squatting in a murder scene without so much as a passing nod to PPE?"

As a medical doctor, one would think the need for personal protective equipment would be hammered into his head so hard during his residency that he'd be putting on gloves and booties in his sleep, but who was I to say? Dr. Yates looked up then and opened his mouth to respond, but I cut him off.

"Or why you're combing through the tatters of the deceased's flesh with what looks like a pen? Or what you think you're doing here at all. No offense there, Doogie, but unless you're telling a detective prelim time of death, cause of death, or to nod and say, 'Why, yes, detective, this was a murder,' there is absolutely no reason you should be anywhere near a body on a scene. Is that clear?"

Yates sputtered as he stood, his expensive-looking loafers squishing in evidence. "Who do you think you are?"

The laugh that came out of my mouth was a whole threat on its own, but the words that followed doubled down on it. "I'm about to be your worst nightmare. Now, you're going to go over to Detective Cooper. He's going to take your clothes, shoes, pen, and anything else he deems necessary for evidence since you tromped all over this place like a bumbling fucking idiot. Then, you are never coming to one of my scenes again, or else I'm going to report you to the state medical board, and you'll have your license taken away so fast they're going to send you back to middle school where you obviously belong."

Yates' face screwed up, clearly insulted. "I'm twenty-six."

It took everything in me not to fly across the corpse between us and slap him upside the head. "Please tell me why out of all the information I just gave you, the slight to your age is all you chose to hear? Get off this crime scene and talk to Detective Cooper. Or don't, and then he can arrest you for obstruction. You choose."

Yates sputtered some more, but I was mentally counting down from ten in my head. If I made it to one, he was getting cuffed, and I didn't care who did it.

"Oh, Dr. Yates?" J called, getting the idiot's attention. "She is neither bluffing nor pulling your leg, and I'd be willing to bet you have less than five seconds before she removes you herself. Do the smart thing and come let me bag your clothes."

"This is ridiculous," Yates griped but moved his ass to the tape, his stupid loafers squishing as he went, repeating his earlier question, "Who the hell do you think you are?"

I only smiled, since I knew J would answer for me, as this wasn't the first person I'd booted from a scene and likely wouldn't be the last.

"She has the highest close rate of any homicide detective in the state. She also has a master's in forensic science from the University of Tennessee with a BS in criminal psychology. And she's Cap's de facto niece, the ADA's daughter, and plays rummy with Judge Peyton. And you're standing on her mother's grave, so I'd move your ass if I were you."

The doctor's face went white as a sheet as he ducked under the tape—which made my lips stretch wider as I gave the small man a little finger wave. I had all my hopes pinned on J stripping him to his skivvies and logging every little bit of it as evidence. And if the idiot had to drive home in his tighty-whities, well, then, all the better.

But as soon as the good doctor was out of sight, I had nothing else to stall with. I let my gaze land on her headstone first as I marveled at the utter absurdity of the dates listed there. According to those bogus dates, my mother was a Gemini, had only been thirty-two when she'd died, and had been a beloved wife and mother. I had little doubt that the whole of the so-called facts etched into the stone were a huge load of bullshit.

Reluctantly, I let my eyes drift once again to my mother's body. Except for the gaping wound at her middle, Mariana appeared untouched. Her face—while a waxy white from blood loss—still sported a painted red lip and impeccable eyeliner, like even in death she willed her makeup to stay put. Save for an errant drop of blood on her cheek, from the shoulders up, she was untouched. The damage done from her shoulders down was a one-way ticket to Nightmare Town, though, and I had a feeling I'd be seeing this scene in my dreams for years to come.

The best I could describe it was as if someone had taken a meat grinder to her or stuffed her full of explosives and set them off. The edges of the wound seemed frayed outward, which wasn't consistent with about a laundry list of possible weapons. Even maulings typically didn't look like this, and I'd seen more than a few of those in my day.

I was at a loss, and I didn't like it one bit.

The swish of booties alerted me to an approach, and I peered up at Bishop's stony face.

"This looks all wrong," he muttered only loud

enough for me to hear. "Not one thing about this fits X's MO."

I couldn't help but agree with him, but I didn't say anything. My wayward brother's modus operandi favored staged deaths that appeared accidental, though his methods were changing. But that wasn't exactly what had me freaking a little bit on the inside.

No, what had me mentally losing my shit was the absence of my mother's pissed-off soul.

A death this bad, this traumatic? Her ghost should be stuck to this body like superglue. Even Hildy was nowhere to be found.

I scanned the surrounding graves, searching for the faint shimmer of specters, my stomach bottoming out when I found none.

"What is it?" Bishop hissed, seeming to scan the crowd with me, even though he couldn't see what I could.

"There aren't any ghosts in this cemetery," I hissed back as I stood, trying to get a better vantage point. In a mild panic, I called to Hildy in my head, yanking him to me like a lasso—or at least I hoped that was what I was doing.

In an instant, my grandfather's ghost appeared before me, his gaze not straying to the corpse at my feet.

His face could only be described as ravaged, the pain seeming to consume him. "I'm here, lass."

A surge of relief nearly made my knees buckle for the second time today, the tears that hit my eyes almost too big to hold in.

"I thought I'd lost you," I whispered, pretending to talk to Bishop so the detectives around us didn't start thinking I was any crazier than I already was.

Shiny tears traced Hildy's cheek as he gave me a solemn nod. "There's something amiss here, lass. Something big. I'll look into it and keep you apprised, but..." He trailed off, his gaze straying to the woman at my feet. "I know she was awful, but she was still mine. I can't be here, lass."

"I understand. Don't go too far, okay?" I hated how needy that sounded, but I refused to give a shit. There was no good reason this cemetery should be empty of ghosts. Not unless...

Not unless X could absorb souls like I could.

Not unless he could consume their energy for power.

Not unless he was just as formidable as I was.

Hildy gave me a grave nod and disappeared, leaving this horrific scene just like I wish I could.

"Please tell me what's going on here," Bishop murmured in my ear.

My whole body felt like a rubber band that had been stretched too tight, unable to snap back like I had before. With the note and Azrael and this, the sheer gruesomeness of the scene and the lack of my mother's soul, the thought of losing Hildy, too, was just too much.

I shook my head. I wanted to tell him, but I knew I'd be setting fire to the very last bit of my reputation if I did—especially here. "Later. When there are less ears, okay?"

Sparing a fleeting glance at Bishop's face, I allowed myself just a little bit of comfort before the rest of the world came crashing down on my head. In it, I saw compassion and kindness and a fierce sort of protectiveness that made me want to kiss him and shove him away all at the same time.

"Anything you need."

I swallowed hard, trying not to lose it. "I need you to find Jimmy for me. He can see shit I can't."

"On it," Bishop muttered, taking off to do just that.

Bishop would get me Jimmy. Jimmy would tell me why my mother's body looked like this. He would tell me all of this was wrong, and it wasn't what I thought, and everything would be okay.

He would.

Or he wouldn't, and I would have to come to terms

with the fact my mother died in the most horrible way imaginable. That was always a possibility, too.

A few minutes later, Jimmy arrived with his camera in tow, his careful gaze assessing everything in front of him. Not a moment passed before he was crooking his finger at me as the hope in my gut died.

Jimmy wasn't going to tell me what I wanted to hear.

Not at all.

5

Jimmy Hanson was the tallest man I'd ever encountered in my life, and that even counted a couple of ghouls I'd met down in Knoxville. Standing at a solid six foot seven, one would never know that he had been relentlessly bullied for being a shrimp in elementary school. Pale-blond hair brushed his shoulders, hiding the very real elf ears underneath.

J and I had taken Jimmy under our wings sometime around third grade at about the time J socked Devon Miller in the nose for knocking Jimmy off the top of the monkey bars. He hunched more around humans than the arcane, his height making him stand out, likely much further than he was comfortable with.

"Please tell me you feel that," he hissed, lifting the

yellow police tape for me to cross. He held out a red biohazard bag for me to drop my booties and gloves before hauling me away from the crowd at large. Being a Fae, Jimmy could see things that I could not—discern shit I could not—so me answering in the negative should not surprise him.

It so did.

"What is on—or rather *who* is on—that grave is not Mariana," he continued. "That is the biggest fucking glamour I have ever seen, and that's saying something."

I blinked at my tall friend, blinked again, and then swiveled to stare at the corpse laid out on my mother's grave. There was no shimmer of spell work, no buzzing of energy. Nothing but a nightmarish scene that I in no way wanted to look at.

And I supposed that was the whole point.

People—even some detectives I knew—didn't stare too long at gruesome scenes, preferring the photos of the periphery rather than the bodies themselves. I tried not to be one of those cops, letting my squeamishness rule my logic, but it hadn't *ever* been a picnic. There had been more than one case to give me nightmares, and that was usually before I was able to talk to their ghosts.

"This whole thing is a ruse," Jimmy continued, bending down to whisper in my ear. "I'll take pictures, but we're going to need to visit the ME's office. I don't know who that is on that grave, but it sure as hell isn't Mariana."

My brain spun out, the possibilities coiling like snakes ready to strike. The two that stuck out the most was that X had planted this body here to throw me off his scent, or... Mariana had to throw X off of hers. I couldn't tell what emotion was flowing through me, but it was definitely *not* relief. Actually, it was a little like rage, a lot like wrath, and with a little sprinkle of betrayal for flavor.

Because it seemed like Mariana was responsible no matter how I looked at it. Just like with her team. Just like Greyson. The bodies seemed to be piling up around her.

Bishop latched onto my forearms, folding them into my body as he and Jimmy moved in what appeared like a choreographed dance, slamming their shoulders together in a wall of man. I didn't get it until I caught the glow of my hands out of the corner of my eye.

Shit.

"I think it's time to go, don't you?" Bishop suggested, not a little amount of abject fear on his face.

Fair enough. If he'd decided to let his arcane freak flag fly in public, I'd probably be looking at him the same way he was staring at me right now.

"Good plan." I met Jimmy's gaze. "Make sure you

and J process the scene like normal. Take pictures, write everything up. I'll meet you at the medical examiner's office."

Jimmy gnashed his teeth but nodded. "Agreed. But be forewarned—Yates is a dick."

Bishop snickered. "Oh, she knows. I'm pretty sure he'll be driving to work in his underwear after what she did to him. Do you really think Cooper bagged all of his clothes?"

That last question was directed at me, and the only thing I could do was wince. If I knew J—and I probably did better than anyone on the planet—making it his life's mission to destroy the good doctor was now etched onto the tippy top of his to-do list.

"Absolutely. And that's being generous."

My least favorite place on the planet—before I spent time in an arcane prison—had always been the medical examiner's office. Typically surrounded by ghosts, and formerly the office of my archnemesis, I made it a point to avoid the place at all costs. Now that Tabitha was toast—courtesy of yours truly—and I knew quite a bit more about myself, the building still wasn't my favorite.

Not by a long shot. For one, it was still surrounded by ghosts, probably still smelled like death, and even though my previous nemesis was likely writhing in Hell, I had a brand-new one to contend with.

At least this one won't be diddling your dad?

That thought had me shuddering as I tried to wipe the image from my brain.

It hadn't taken too long for J and Jimmy to process the scene after my departure. With the lack of weird woo-woo shit—other than the half-exploded body, of course—there was little to catalogue, which left the majority of the examination to the good Dr. Yates.

As much as I would *love* trying to get on the good side of that asshole so I could get access to the body, that actually wasn't what I dreaded at the moment. Before we went in there, I would have to tell Hildy the truth, and that was what had me stalling in my Jeep while I stared at ghosts loitering at the building's entrance.

Bishop sat in the driver's seat, his fingers laced with mine as I stared out the windshield. I didn't know when I'd become a sucker for a good hand hold, or when precisely I'd turned into a thirteen-year-old girl with a crush, but holding Bishop's hand in my car was just about the best thing I had going for me right then.

Naturally, he opened his big mouth and ruined it.

"You have to tell him, you know. That it isn't her."

I rolled my eyes and my head on the headrest,

shooting him a glare. "I will," I insisted petulantly, "but he's going to end up just as pissed as I am, and I don't exactly know what he'll do. My gut does not say good things about this situation and..." I trailed off, unwilling to say what was racing in my head.

Hell, I didn't even want to be thinking this shit, let alone saying it.

"What situation?" Hildy asked from my back seat, scaring the ever-loving fuck out of me.

I also may or may not have squeaked like a puppy's chew toy in fright. "Jesus, fuck, Hildenbrand. Warn a girl next time, will ya?"

Hildy ignored me, repeating, "What situation are you referring to, lass?"

I shot Bishop a worried glance before just coming out with it. "The situation where the body on Mariana's grave is not Mariana."

Wincing, I prepared for the outburst in three... two... one...

"What?" That lone word had all the hair on my arms standing at attention. Hildy hadn't yelled it, either, and that made it all the worse.

"Jimmy said it was a glamour—a big one."

"It would fucking well have to be, wouldn't it?" Hildy seethed in his seat, his form flickering back and forth between solid and transparent like a damn strobe light. "Do you know what is required for a working that big? To get the details exactly right?"

I didn't, but I had a feeling he was going to tell me. Instead of spilling the beans, Hildy vanished from my car only to appear at the building's entrance, his rage making him flicker in and out of sight in broad daylight.

Bishop and I scrambled out of the car. What we thought we were going to do, I had no idea. It was one thing to bitch slap a ghost I didn't know, but this was Hildy. Sure, I had contemplated punting his cantankerous ass into the next realm a time or two, but this was different.

"What the fuck, Hildy?" I hissed, my gaze skittering around to see if there was anyone to witness my grandfather losing his shit in the middle of the damn day.

Bishop nudged me right as Hildy went transparent once more. I whipped my head up to see Yates barreling down the sidewalk toward us. Dressed in a set of navy-blue scrubs, the flinty blue to his eyes seemed to glow with wrath.

"I know you aren't here to see that body, Adler," he announced like a threat.

Oh, so he's finally learned my name. Yippee.

Dr. Yates didn't stop at the appropriate distance for polite conversation, either. Oh, no. This little pipsqueak decided invading my personal space was a good idea. Unfortunately for him, he was about two inches shorter than I was, so it was me staring down at him like he'd lost his mind.

"Got the best close record in the state, do you? Well, I'll make it so you never close another case again." Spittle landed on my cheek right around the time Bishop's hand—with not a little "umph" behind it—shoved into Yates' chest.

"Threatening to obstruct justice with a witness present doesn't seem to be in your best interests, Doc. I suggest you settle down before I make you," Bishop growled, stepping in front of me.

"Protecting your girlfriend, I see. And what are you going to do about it?" Yates taunted.

Every muscle in Bishop's back tensed like he was about to smite the idiot on the sidewalk.

But Bishop never got the chance.

No, that mantle was taken up by my grandfather who decided appearing in front of this asshole was the best idea in his fool brain.

"Nothing," Hildy threatened, his solid body and glowing skull cane looming over the man. "He doesn't have to. But I can and I will do something about you if you don't start acting right. And there's not a damn thing you can do about it."

At the sight of Hildy appearing out of thin air, Yates' face went white. His slate-blue eyes rounded as he stumbled back, pressing himself to the building's façade.

"You're... you're... you can't..." Yates stuttered, cowering from Hildy like a child while I racked my brain to figure out the best course of action.

I only had two options, and both sucked. I could either screech at Hildy like a loon, or I could pretend I didn't see anything at all. While I much preferred Dr. Yates to think he was having a mental break, that just seemed wrong to me. Too bad the good doctor didn't give me any time to ride to his rescue. As soon as he found his footing, Yates raced for the doors of the building, practically leaving smoke trails in his wake.

"That's what I thought, ya yellow bastard," Hildy taunted, calling at Yates' back like a schoolyard bully. "Run like the coward you are!" Then he started bocking like a chicken, doing the whole arm-flapping, feet wiggle thing to boot.

It was all I could do to not dissolve into the pavement. "Knock it the fuck off, Hildy. You're going to get me in trouble."

Bishop's shoulders started shaking before he was doubled over in laughter.

"Some help you are. I thought keeping the arcane away from humans was your whole fucking job." I mean,

I was going to have to work with this asshole and every time he saw me, he would flip the fuck out. Add that to the budding grudge, and my work environment was about to be toxic as fuck.

Bishop wiped tears from his eyes as he straightened. "It is, but Yates isn't human, so I don't feel anything but a supreme sort of joy at watching him almost piss himself. Good work, O'Shea. Punching him in the face would have been far too much paperwork."

Yates wasn't human?

Was anyone in this damn town?

6

"**D**id I just see what I thought I did?" J asked as he climbed the steps to the medical examiner's office, Jimmy just behind him.

I shot a glare at Hildy—who was once again his usual transparent—and shook my head. "If you saw Hildy threatening the new ME, then yes, it was exactly what you thought it was."

J blinked at me, wide-eyed, but Jimmy started snickering. Jimmy was kind to everyone, so for him to revel in someone else's discomfort, it meant the good doctor had been a Grade-A asshole to my favorite elf.

"Please tell me someone got it on video," Jimmy said, rubbing his hands together like a Viking-style Mr. Burns. "I would pay money to see that again."

That had me scanning the roofline for CCTV

cameras. Several of the municipal buildings had them, but I had no idea if this particular building was wired, too. I was able to breathe a sigh of relief after I tamped down the urge to flick everyone in their ear. Sure, this side of the building and street weren't a hotbed of activity, but it wasn't like it was secluded, either.

"Sorry to disappoint," I scolded, "but, no, we didn't." No offense to Jimmy, but I had already spent nearly a year in an arcane prison, and I had no desire for a return visit. After the close call out at Dove Creek, the thought of exposing the arcane to humans made me nauseous.

"Pity," he muttered. "Yates has been a pain in everyone's ass since Tabitha went on her little walkabout." We both knew that Tabitha was dead as a doornail, but that was neither here nor there. "Damn warlocks. I swear that whole species makes mages look well-adjusted—no offense," he said, giving Bishop an apprehensive smile.

"None taken," Bishop assured him.

"Anyway, Mike should be ahead of us, so we should go in before that asshole has time to screw something else up."

Mike Harmon was the assistant medical examiner and probably the nicest man on the planet. He was one of those people who had a smile and a kind word for just about everyone. Though his genial nature did make me question his sanity sometimes. I mean, who functions that well on no sleep, no food, and nary a coffee IV to be found anywhere?

Psychopaths, that's who.

I cut my eyes to Hildy. "Behave or you're going home, got it?"

Hildy gave me an unrepentant smile and winked out of sight.

Yeah, he was going to do no such thing.

Grumbling, I followed him in the building, hoping to stop whatever torture shenanigans he had planned for Yates. The absolute last thing I needed was that idiot's death on my conscience. But when I stepped fully into the corridor, where I was, and *what* I was smacked me in the face.

The last time I'd been to this building was nearly a year ago. Before prison. Before I learned who I was. It was before Tabitha tried to murder my dad.

No, Darby, she did not try anything. She killed him right in front of you.

Flashes of his death, of the warmth of his blood on my hands, of the light dying in his eyes, hit me with the force of a wrecking ball. And that was before I mentally dealt with the fact that this building was ghost fucking central.

Just like before, the wide hallway was teeming with

specters, though most of them were keeping their distance this time. The one who didn't was a little boy that appeared no older than seven. His sweet face and dark curls made my heart melt into the floor as he reached for my hand like any lost child would.

"Can you help me find my mommy?" he said, and my eyes welled up with tears.

Had I ever been this small, this trusting? Had I loved my mom this much?

At the touch of his hand, I learned his name was Elijah, and he'd died sometime in the 1930s from a bad fall. He'd been playing in a tree and climbed on a dying branch by accident. If he'd passed ninety years ago, his mother was likely just as dead as he was.

All I could do was nod in answer, pulling him into me as the flavor of his life burst through my head. He'd been loved and cared for, the memories of his mother's smile stinging like a slap. I couldn't help but be envious of this child—envious and glad that he was getting peace after wandering alone for so long.

I mentally called out my thanks to the specters waiting in the hallway, the ache in my chest at so many waiting souls almost too much for me to bear. That child had been waiting nearly ninety years. Ninety. Almost a century of being scared and unable to find his family.

Azrael, if you're looking for souls to reap, this is the place. I can't take them all.

I figured I could take about five before I started looking like a walking, talking Edison bulb.

"What are you doing?" Bishop asked in my ear, his arm wrapping around my middle from behind.

"This place is still full of souls. I thought when Tabitha..." I trailed off, not wanting to go on. Swallowing, I sallied forth. "I thought when she was gone, what was keeping them here would go away. But they're all still here. And I can't save them all."

I didn't add that if I tried, I'd burn up and die. That little fact was implied.

Bishop's arm tightened, the squeeze of support bolstering me far more than I thought it would. "We'll fix it, but right now we have a job to do."

All I could do was nod. Bishop was right. I needed to know who was on that grave. I needed to stop Hildy from torturing the new ME. I needed to find my brother and stop him from killing people.

Preferably not in that order.

I'll come back. I'll fix this.

But the truth was that fixing this mess might be too much for me to handle. I'd thought when Tabitha had collected the souls to raise Azrael that we'd gotten them all, but it seemed like I'd barely scratched the surface. And I couldn't help them—not and stay alive, anyway.

Swallowing hard, I broke from Bishop's hold, heading straight for the examination room, pushing through the swinging doors as I braced myself for the smell.

No matter how good the refrigeration or air filtration, this building had always smelled like dead things. I mean, it made sense, but that didn't do my nose any favors. Upon entering the room, I was immediately accosted with the scent of lemon balm and rosemary—not necessarily unpleasant, but odd to smell in a lab.

Dr. Yates was tossing handfuls of salt at Hildy as the deceased grave talker continued to bock at him like a chicken.

Salt? Lemon balm and rosemary? This guy really is a warlock.

"Oh, knock it the fuck off, Hildy," I commanded, using every bit of my power to make my ghostly grandfather act his damn age. "I can't get anything out of him if he's scared into hysterics, now, can I?"

Instantly, Hildy quit his taunting, shooting me a petulant glare before he went transparent again.

"This blithering idiot was threatening you. It is my

grandfatherly duty to give him nightmares until the end of time. You're spoiling my fun, lass."

I rolled my eyes before pinching my brow. "And then we'll have to deal with a whole new ME, and we know my track record with those. Just quit it. If he continues to be an ass, then you can make his life hell. I'll even give you my blessing."

Hildy's smile was practically diabolical as Yates' face went from white to positively gray.

"You... you can still see him? Is he a... a...?"

At this rate, my eyes were just going to roll on out of my head. "A ghost?"

Yates nodded vigorously, still plastered to the wall like a damn barnacle, holding his jar of salt like it would do anything.

Ghosts aren't demons. Idiot.

"Yeah. You know this whole building is teeming with them, right? I mean, you work with the dead every day. Did you think they just left?" Bishop had said he was an arcaner, but damn. I'd never seen one so freaked at the thought of a little spirit. True, Hildy was nothing to sneeze at, but still.

"Oh, don't break his brain," Jimmy advised. "This is the same guy who uses lemon balm for odor control instead of an actual spell." The elf plopped his giant self down on a rolling stool as he shot Yates a withering glance.

"I thought you said he was a warlock?" J asked, assessing the ME with his speculating gaze. I knew hardened criminals who couldn't withstand that look.

"I am," Yates grumbled, peeling himself from the wall. "But I don't use my magic unless I have to. It's a good way to get yourself thrown in a dark hole somewhere."

"More like you don't have any magic to use," Jimmy shot back. "You have a ton of trapped souls just teeming in here and you've done nothing. I offered to help cleanse this place, and what did you say?"

"Like I was going to accept help from a Fae." Yates sneered. "I'd rather not be enslaved, thank you very much."

Jimmy sneered right back, but it was J who looked like he was close to punching Yates right in the face. "How about you watch your mouth," he warned, "before I come over there and make you."

J had been protecting Jimmy since we were kids, sure, but never had he looked that close to losing it as an adult.

"Aww, you got yourself a pet. How sweet," Yates said sarcastically, and Jimmy had to bodily hold J back before he hauled off and lost his damn mind.

"See," Hildy griped. "I could have made the bastard piss himself, but *noooo. He's too fragile. We might need him.* Need him like a hole in the head."

I searched the ceiling for patience. Finding none, I abandoned the squabbling men to search for the body I'd braved this damn building for. Donning gloves by rote, I then started opening the refrigerated slab drawers, one by one, until I found a black body bag with today's date.

Bishop did the honors of unzipping the bag, a task I dreaded on all the levels. Those damn things held in smells, fluids, and everything else, and I was not too keen on them being unleashed on the room. But before he had his hand on the zippered tab for more than a microsecond, Yates was in his face.

"Do not touch that body," the young doctor scolded, and that's right about the time Bishop lost what little patience he had left.

"Then how about you do your damn job?" Bishop growled, letting just a hint of his other side leak out of his eyes. "So far today, I have seen you damage evidence, threaten a police officer, and obstruct an investigation. I have yet to see you do your actual profession."

I was so over all of this. I was over Yates' sniping, and J and Jimmy's antagonism, and Bishop and Hildy's blustering.

I was just done. At this point it wasn't just about me and my discomfort. It wasn't about what I had gone through or what respect I'd earned. It was about this poor woman who had likely done nothing other than being in the wrong place at the wrong time.

"Does anyone care that there is a woman dead on that slab? Does anyone care that she has no spirit, no soul for me to send on? Does no one give a shit about her?" I didn't add that at this point I didn't even know who she was. I knew who she'd been glamoured to be, but without Jimmy removing it, I didn't know a damn thing about her.

And if I didn't know anything about her, I couldn't solve her fucking murder.

"The woman in that bag is wearing my mother's face. Was spread out on her grave. Do any of you give that first fuck about that?" I stared at each of their faces in turn, and even Yates seemed appropriately abashed. "All this sniping bullshit stops right now. Do you hear me?"

Without a word, Yates took the zipper in hand and revealed a nightmare.

7

The sight of my mother's waxy pale face emerging from the black body bag made my entire body lurch. I trusted Jimmy. I did. But seeing was believing, and all I saw was her blonde hair stained with blood, her cornflower blue eyes open and unseeing.

I was only capable of a stiff upper lip for so long before I broke, and that breaking point was fast approaching.

"You're sure this is a glamour?" I asked, the shattered question coming out before I could stop it.

I shouldn't give that first fuck about Mariana O'Shea. She was a complicit murderer, a conniving sneak. She was the fucking worst.

But still...

Still, I remembered what she had been like when I was a child, and I hated that she'd hidden so well under the guise of a good mom.

Because a good mom wouldn't hang you out to dry.

A good mom wouldn't send you to prison.

A good mom wouldn't have you tortured for nearly a year to keep from blowing her cover.

Mariana wasn't a good mom. She wasn't a good person.

I should hate her.

But I didn't.

"I am one hundred percent positive that is not Mariana. The cloaking is quite impressive, sure, but I can still see through it."

Jimmy's answer did little in the way of reassuring me, despite the conviction in his tone. Childhood trauma, party of one?

A part of me wanted to snipe, to lash out, wanted to tell him to get the lead out. The other part didn't want to know who was under that mask, even if that made me a monster, too.

"What kind of glamour are we talking about here?" Bishop asked, his fingers finding mine and squeezing them tight in support. "An Oslov Webbing or—"

"No," Jimmy insisted, cutting him off. "An Oslov even you would feel. This is a Morana."

At Jimmy's grave pronouncement, Hildy hissed. My ghostly grandfather shook his head as Jimmy continued.

"A Morana requires a sacrifice. One of an innocent. Usually a child. Only experienced practitioners can even attempt it, though most do not. The Morana has been outlawed for centuries, though some Fae still use it. It is how they stay hidden from humans."

From what I'd gathered in my limited time with the arcane was that the Fae were a whole other breed. Not exactly arcaners, not exactly human. They came not from this earth but from cracks in the veil. Our rules seemed trite to them, seemed almost cute. Though the same could be said for other species. What a vampire or a shifter deemed appropriate may seem like straight murder everywhere else. The same could be said about demons or spirits or any other facet of the arcane. Humans, too. What was allowed centuries ago would seem practically barbaric today.

Still, sacrificing an innocent so you could hide was far more than I could stomach, and I hoped Mariana couldn't possibly be that cruel.

Yeah, yeah. I'm an optimist or whatever.

"Can you break the working?" I asked, not looking at the dead woman wearing my mother's face or Jimmy and instead staring at Hildy. Hildy knew something. I could feel it in my bones.

At feeling my stare, he met my gaze. "He's being kind to ya, lass. Sparing ya. A Morana requires a newborn baby as a sacrifice. It's why they are so powerful."

I shot a look at Jimmy and then Bishop. By their expressions, both of them knew what it really meant. Both of them knew that it was a possibility that my mother had... had...

"No," I whispered, bile crawling up my throat. "There's no way she would..." But I didn't finish because Bishop's face said it all.

It said that not only would Mariana murderer a newborn baby to save her own skin, but she'd done a lot worse.

I wanted to vomit.

But more? I wanted to know who the hell was under that glamour so I could get some clues to find the bitch.

"Don't do that," I warned Bishop. "Don't you dare try to spare me from this shit. Do you understand me? That doesn't do me any favors. All it does is keep me in the dark."

I gave J my full attention because, just like me, he was in the dark. "What they're not saying is that one of the ingredients for the spell is a newborn baby's death. Not a child. A fucking baby. You know, just in case you thought there was a redeemable thing about any of this shit." I turned to Jimmy and repeated my earlier question. "Can you break it?"

Jimmy's jaw tightened, likely in affront, but I didn't care. J had to know what he was walking into just like I did. He had to see that this world—this dark, cold world—was far more dangerous than he could comprehend. I trusted Jimmy. I did. I even trusted Bishop. But there were plenty of arcaners out there that he shouldn't trust.

"I think so," he replied, affixing his gaze on the dead woman. "But you should stand back."

Yates, to his credit, finally started listening to Jimmy and bolted for the farthest corner of the room. I didn't move so much as an inch until Bishop's fingers tightened on my hand and he drew me away, tucking me behind his back just to be extra careful. Out of the two of us, I was probably less fragile, but I wasn't going to argue with him. He'd put himself in front of me in the middle of a damn vampire's nest, for fuck's sake. We both knew his mental faculties were suspect.

Jimmy looked down at J, who also hadn't made any attempt to move. "I'm not playing with you about this. Get behind me or get out of this room."

"Who's going to protect you?" J asked, and my heart did a little flutter, which I didn't think was possible in this situation.

Jimmy dropped a kiss to J's lips—which again with

the flutter—and shook his head. "Haven't you figured it out yet? I've never needed protecting. I just like it when you do it. Now get behind me? Please?"

J pursed his lips like he was thinking about it but moved behind him, anyway.

In the next instant, Jimmy's hands began to glow, shooting off gold sparks every few seconds. Slowly, he brought his arms down, his fingers making contact with the dead woman's skin. The lights in the room began to flicker as a vibration from the floor rattled my bones. Bishop backed up a step, pushing me against the wall of refrigerated slabs, the metal door handle digging in my back. The suspended fluorescent lights swung to and fro as they flickered, and all the while, Jimmy clenched his jaw like he was in pain. The vibrations simmered down just as quickly as they came on, and I thought the worst was over. I was proven wrong not a second later when wind whipped through the closed room as the doors to the other slabs began rattling. The floor pitched, and had Bishop not braced himself against me, I would have been knocked on my ass.

Yates—having no protection—wasn't so lucky. He fell like a sack of potatoes but still maintained the wherewithal to at least hide under his desk.

Ceiling tiles hit the floor, exploding on impact as the

transom windows above the swinging doors cracked. They, too, shattered not a second later.

Then just as quickly as it started, it stopped.

I braved a peek around Bishop's shoulder. "Everyone okay?"

Hildy spoke up first. "Fine, lass. Tell that Fae friend of yours not to do that anymore. From here on out, we're doing sketches instead."

I couldn't disagree.

Bishop didn't answer. He only peeled himself off of me and held out his hand. I figured he needed the reassurance I was okay. Either that, or he wanted a hand on me in the event he needed to shade jump me out of here. J only shot me a wide-eyed stare. Granted, I doubted we'd seen even a fraction of Jimmy's power, but that shit was impressive.

Then my gaze fell on the body bag and the woman inside it. She had red hair and pale skin, sharp features, and a mulish mouth even in her final rest.

And unfortunately, I knew her.

I couldn't recall her name—given I'd only met her once—but I couldn't forget her if I tried. The last time I'd seen this woman's face, she'd been casually discussing my imminent death. She was a Knoxville coven witch.

Karen? Courtney? Kat? Katrina. That was it. She was

one of Shiloh's lieutenants or something.

My old friend dread started making a home in my gut. I was going to have to talk to Shiloh, tell her that her friend was dead. But more than that, Shiloh had done me dirty the last time we spoke, and it hadn't been a little thing, either. She hadn't just stepped on my toes. She'd screwed me over on an epic scale. I'd gotten nothing out of the sleeper agent masquerading as an ABI agent because of her. I was stuck with my ass blowing in the wind because she wanted revenge.

And now her coven sister was dead.

It would be better if I had something—anything—to go on, but I didn't even have Katrina's ghost to question. I had approximately fuck all, and I had to walk into the coven headquarters?

I might as well just ask my father to come take me because I was ten steps past fucked.

"We know her," J muttered, staring at the same face that had been so callous about our imminent deaths nearly a year ago.

"She is—or rather, was—in the Knoxville coven. Katrina, I think." I shut my eyes and called to this poor woman's spirit in my mind, pleading for it to come to me. As I figured the case to be, I got nothing. "She doesn't have a spirit hanging around, and yes, Hildy, I already tried calling to it. What if..."

What if it had already been reaped? I didn't say that question out loud, but I could tell Hildy was thinking it, too.

"She shouldn't be able to do what you do, lass. Not like that. If it was your mother, then she would just drain the spirit, not send it off to her rest. We should still be able to access her unless the poor thing has already moved on."

"I'd better not get fired for this," Bishop grumbled under his breath, shaking his head as black swirls of magic raced up his arms.

In the next instant, Katrina sat up, her bloody wide-open maw of a torso peeking out of the body bag as her head slowly turned to stare at him. Her blue eyes filmed over with white, her mouth falling open in an imitation of how it would in life. She drew in a ragged breath, a shudder racking her body as if in death she could get a chill.

"Katrina of the Knoxville coven, I call you forth," Bishop commanded, his speech formal as his magic weaved over her reanimated body. "Tell me the circumstances of your death. Tell me who killed you."

A creepy-as-fuck smile bloomed on her face, but she said nothing. Instead, her seemingly unseeing eyes found me.

Those milky-white orbs felt like they burned me as

her lips widened further, the unnatural smile like a predator.

Katrina dragged in a breath, filling her long-dead lungs, and then she began to speak.

"You saved him once, but Death has him in his sights," she hissed, her words like ice running in my veins. Without so much as a millisecond to ponder it, I knew exactly who she was talking about.

With Bishop's help, I'd brought my father back from the dead. Given him another chance at life as I'd taken another's.

It took everything I had in me to stay still, to not react, because my gut said that this wasn't Katrina speaking. No, this was like a prerecorded message just for me.

"I wonder if you can keep him alive this time. I wonder if your real father will help you save your fake one. Tick tock, child. Death is waiting."

At that parting statement, Katrina's body wilted. The spell left her as quickly as it came, her head smacking the slab with a sickening thud.

But I barely heard any of it.

Without another thought in my brain, I turned and ran.

8

The arm banding around my middle pissed me the fuck off. I needed to get to my dad. I needed to make sure he was okay. I needed to keep him alive.

But also, I wasn't an idiot. The fact that this was most certainly a trap flashed like a neon sign in my brain.

Why else had that body been programmed with that message?

But before I could say a word and before I could land my quasi-boyfriend on his ass, the light in the hallway seemed to fade, and then the whole of the world sped up. My stomach nearly lurched out of my body as Bishop hauled me through space and time, the world screaming to a stop in the middle of my father's office. Papers fluttered, books rattled on their shelves, but I didn't see any of it.

No, I was too busy scrambling for the wastepaper basket as the tacos Bishop so graciously brought to me made a *spectacular* reappearance.

"What the hell is going on?" Dad shouted, but I barely heard him over my heaving.

Fuck shade jumping. Fuck Bishop. Fuck this day. Just fuck. It. All.

I heard my father's bar fridge open and close, and a bottle of water landed squarely in my line of sight. I dove for it, chugging breathtakingly cool water like my life depended on it.

"A threat was made on your life, Killian. I have no doubt it's a trap, but I think we need to get you out of here." Bishop's clear, concise answer was vague enough that I had no doubt this wasn't the first time he'd had to inform someone that their life was in danger.

"What the hell are you talking about?"

"Not here," I croaked, managing to get myself under control. "I promise I'll tell you everything, but we have to get the hell out of this office."

Please, Azrael, please keep him safe. Please don't let anything happen to him.

Was I an idiot for asking my birth father for help on the same damn day I'd scolded him? Probably.

Was I still hoping he'd be there to save my ass? Absolutely.

But I had no expectations when it came to Azrael. He was a wildcard, an unknown, and we owed nothing to each other.

"Take him," I urged Bishop. "Take him somewhere no one will find him."

The clench of Bishop's jaw told me he would be doing nothing of the sort. "There is no guarantee that he isn't being tracked. That this isn't just one big trap."

"Trap?" Dad growled, his hands clenching into fists.

I opened my mouth to explain, but before I could say another word, J and Jimmy raced into the room, the pair of them puffing like they'd sprinted the whole way here. I had to admit, I would have taken the run over puking in my dad's wastebasket after shade jumping.

At the utter lack of death, destruction, or even a good maiming, J rested his hands on his knees and dropped his head. "That. Sucked. It's too damn hot to run that fast."

I didn't have a good feeling about any of this. My dad was fine. Wasn't he?

"I don't get it," Jimmy muttered. "I don't see

anything in this office. No spells, no wardings, no nothing."

"It's because there aren't any," Hildy hissed in my ear, making me jump. "This was a diversion, plain and simple."

I didn't want to say it, but Hildy was making a hell of a lot of sense.

"Anyone with a brain in their head knows how much I love my dad. Anyone—X, Mariana, a man out on the street—would know that I would do anything to keep my dad alive. Yes, it's a diversion, but from what?"

What had I been planning on doing before my father's life was threatened? Visiting the coven house to let them know Katrina had been murdered.

My dad needed protection, yes, but I needed to press on. I wasn't going to let that asshole David Copperfield this shit on me. But I had no idea where to keep my dad. It felt wrong to think it because he was a grown-ass man, but he was vulnerable, and because he was, I was too.

"How about I go to Dave's for a few days?" Dad offered. "Leave Hildy with me in case things go sideways, and I'll keep my head down."

It made so much sense, I wanted to cry. Before I could think twice about it, I practically attack-hugged my dad. I hoped he knew what I was feeling—that him staying safe, that him doing his best to stay out of this whirlwind of shit was all I needed to get my head in the game.

After Tabitha, I just couldn't risk his life again. I couldn't leave him unprotected.

"Your dad has a good head on his shoulders," Hildy said, his voice pitched soft like he was handling me with kid gloves. "Tell him I'd be honored to keep watch. I promise to come to ya if there is any danger."

I nodded into my father's chest. "Hildy says he's in."

And then it dawned on me that Dad didn't know about Mariana.

"Also, there's something I need to tell you..."

"I've never seen your dad's face turn that color," J marveled from my back seat.

"Yes, you have, don't lie." I shook my head as I flipped my turn signal on. "Remember the superglue incident when we were twelve?"

"Is this the time you 'accidentally' superglued J's hat to his head?" Jimmy snickered. "Because I remember that you had to shave your head, and your mom was pissed. Then your mom called her dad, and then it was a whole mess."

"To my credit, J wanted to shave his head. I just gave him a motive. Also, Corrine couldn't prove it was me."

Mainly because it hadn't been. It had been J the whole time. I just took the wrap.

"A criminal as a pre-teen, Adler. I'm shocked. Shocked, I tell you." Bishop chuckled.

I was glad we were all laughing and pretending life was all peaches and roses. It made me less likely to hurl from nerves. We were on our way to the Knoxville coven house, and I was not looking forward to telling Shiloh that she'd lost a sister. Nor that my she-beast of a mother was likely involved. Or that this had to do with my brother somehow.

Okay, I probably wasn't going to tell her some of that —mostly because I didn't quite trust her anymore.

"Have you heard from Sarina?" I asked, changing the subject. Yes, I'd been a hellion, but I'd straightened myself out in the end.

"Just a text saying to keep watch on you. As far as assignments go, I'm not mad at it."

Coming from Sarina, that kind of suggestion had an ominous flair to it. Especially since the ABI had been radio silent since they were breached a few days prior. Bishop said it was protocol, but I wasn't convinced. Nor was I convinced that Sarina was just taking some time off.

I knew something was up—I just didn't have the courage to ask. Everything felt up in the air, unsettled, and I didn't know how to make it right again.

Or if that was even my job.

Somehow, it felt like it was.

We entered Knoxville just as the sun was setting, making our task all the more dangerous. I was about to make shit real tense for a coven on the eve of the full moon, and I was not looking forward to it.

Mostly, I was worried about how Shiloh would take it —losing a member of her coven. A year ago, I could have predicted exactly how my friend would react, but with her actions at the Dubois nest, I couldn't be so sure now.

"Sarina would text us if she saw my imminent death, right?"

I felt Bishop's sharp stare on my cheek as I navigated the city streets, but I didn't return it.

"Of course she would," he said carefully, his words a measured cadence of potential bullshit. "If Sarina thought you were in danger, she's likely to insert herself right in the middle of this mess without a second's hesitation. The reason she's a supervisor baffles me on the daily."

We rode the rest of the way to the coven house in silence, Bishop's careful words boring a hole in my brain, and the variables in just this one task alone made me want to pack a bag for a deserted island and call it a day.

I couldn't help the feeling that something horrible was about to happen.

The Knoxville coven house was actually a historical mansion in Knoxville's arcane district. The humans themselves never knew that the arcane walked among them. Still, this city—just like many others in the world —held hidden secrets. Respective sides of town that humans did not traverse and had no idea even existed. Places that urged them to keep driving, keep moving.

The Dubois nest made their home on one side of the cordoned-off arcane district and the coven on the other, the sprawling white mansion standing like an aging lady, proud and resilient. Like the Dubois nest, the coven house projected an air of doom and death. I wasn't fooled by the pretty columns and giant veranda. This house had just as much death, just as much blood tied to it as the decommissioned cathedral.

And just as many ghosts.

There was a good reason I tried to meet Shiloh at coffee shops and my own safe spaces. Places where I knew the wards were tuned specifically to keep specters out. Witches were ghost magnets—especially the ones who dealt in ancestral magics. The carefully clipped lawn leading up to the door was littered with spirits, each of them staring at the house like they would love to come in but couldn't.

For a grave talker, I wasn't exactly comfortable with a slew of specters just chilling in my general vicinity— especially this close to nightfall. And unlike the ones at the ME's office, these lovely people likely had no idea they were dead.

I had big enough fish to fry without dealing with this mess, and I wasn't going to tackle it if I had a way around it.

"Please tell me you feel that," Bishop muttered, his jaw like stone.

If the man meant the buzz of roughly fifty souls just chilling, then yes. "Yup. I'm going to pretend I can't see this shit as I walk on past if you don't mind."

"That's what that is?" J asked, shivering as he rubbed his arms, the warm spring dusk nothing against the chill of the dead.

I nodded my head, marching down the cobblestone sidewalk with a purpose.

Before we reached the picketed gate, I spied a slight woman with a head full of wavy black hair barring our way. Her dark eyes narrowed when they landed on us, her hands making a home on her hips as a scowl pulled at her lips.

"I thought I told you to keep her safe. What part of heading to a house full of witches on the night of the full moon sounds safe to you?" Sarina addressed Bishop as she enfolded me into a hug. "I swear, I can't leave you two alone for a minute."

She let me go and passed out her Sarina hugs to Bishop, J, and Jimmy.

"And I told you that she was a grown woman who could make her own decisions, and I was not going to fall for that bullshit trap."

I had to fight off the urge to kiss him right in the middle of this sidewalk in front of everyone.

"Oohhh, brownie points," Sarina cooed, more than likely reading my thoughts.

Rolling my eyes, I directed my attention to Jimmy and J.

"Want me to watch your six?" J asked before I could say anything.

I nodded. "I have a bad feeling shit is about to go down. Maybe if I don't roll up with the whole gang in tow, I can keep it copacetic."

Add in the fact that the lone human wouldn't be in the thick of the shit if it did decide to pop off.

"We'll be here."

Gathering my courage, I opened the gate and

stomped down the path toward the coven's front door, ignoring the clusters of spirits and my gut.

In hindsight, ignoring my gut was a mistake.

Just as I was climbing the steps to the veranda, the front door opened, a stone-faced Shiloh on the other side.

"You're not supposed to be here," she hissed, and then all hell broke loose.

9

When the coven leader of Knoxville decided you were no longer welcome on her property, there were only two options you could take.

The first option: run. *Smart, a solid plan, and a real contender for keeping a person such as myself breathing.*

The problem was with the second option, which had been ingrained in my head since my father told me I couldn't have the Oreos when I was four, sticking them on top of the refrigerator to keep them out of reach. As soon as someone told me I couldn't be somewhere, shouldn't do this thing, couldn't do something, immediately that was all I wanted to do. I got those damn Oreos, and I was staying right where I was.

It's a sickness, I know.

Shiloh St. James stood between us and her house, her arms loose at her sides like she could throw a spell at any second. Her expression practically screamed pissed-off mama cat as the air around her seemed to shimmer.

She was going to attack me. My friend, my arcane confidant, my ally, was going to hurt me because I showed up unannounced.

Yeah, that's not suspicious.

"Right?" I shot back, trying to diffuse the situation. "I should be on vacation, having wild, sweaty sex with this guy," I said, hooking a thumb at Bishop, "but I'm on your damn doorstep. Obviously, my plans changed. You and I need to talk."

Shiloh's perfectly arched eyebrows rose on her forehead as her stance relaxed a bit. She let out a soft, husky chuckle. "Is that right? You bring the ABI to *my* damn doorstep and have the nerve to be angry at me?"

I gritted my teeth. "Do you think I would be here if it wasn't fucking dire? I'm passing up yummy death mage sex for your ass. Get with the program."

I practically felt the heat of Bishop's stare on my whole body like the sweetest of caresses.

At least someone is listening to me.

Then two things happened at once.

The specters on the lawn seemed to flicker, their

silvery-gray forms winking in and out like a burning out lightbulb, and the door behind Shiloh opened.

Three women filed out of the house behind their coven leader.

One of them wearing Katrina's face.

Before I could eke out that there was a traitor in Shiloh's midst, Not-Katrina volleyed a spell at me. A blistering arrow of light rocketed toward me faster than I could track as I reached for the gun that I'd so foolishly surrendered to Cap. Coming up empty, I barely managed to dive to the side just as the heat of the working grazed my arm.

I hit the grass, reaching for my backup weapon, the training so ingrained that I didn't even think to use the power coursing through my body.

Bishop had no such compunction.

Black and purple swirls of magic raced up his arms as shadows fell over the already-darkening sky. Sarina stood right beside him, a gun in her hand.

I was loath to use a gun with witches involved, but I would if I had to. Sarina seemed to be of the same mind, her hesitation at firing clear as day.

A spell flew from Bishop's fingertips, slamming into Not-Katrina with the force of a wrecking ball. She soared through the air, her body colliding with the wood siding with a terrible crack. The redheaded witch still managed to land on her feet, though, her green eyes ignoring the man who made her fly like a kite and narrowing at me in particular.

A ball of white flames bloomed in her hand as she gave me a sneering smile. A sneering smile I knew well enough, just on another woman's face. I was willing to bet my whole pension that I knew who was wearing Katrina's skin.

The weight of the gun in my hand made everything slow to a crawl, the ball of magic sailing through the air at a snail's pace. Without a second's hesitation, I aimed and squeezed the trigger. The recoil ricocheted through my arms as I watched the bullets rocket toward their intended target. Not-Katrina held up a hand as she whispered a word I couldn't hear. And while my aim was true, those bullets curved at the last second, skirting around the witch and hitting the façade behind her.

I wasn't the only one firing, either. Sarina squeezed off five shots herself, each one landing anywhere but where she aimed them. The wall behind Not-Katrina was Swiss cheese by the time we got the message that bullets weren't going to do a damn thing.

Black and purple orbs of magic collided midair with two flaming balls of light, the concussion of spells making the whole of the world shake.

But that wasn't the worst part.

No, the worst part was those ghosts that I had been so staunchly ignoring had turned as one to stare at me.

That's when I knew for certain who was wearing Katrina's face. Only a grave talker had that much control over the dead. Only a grave talker could wield them like a sword.

And only a grave talker could turn those ghosts into a weapon.

Pressure popped in my ears as I felt a ghost turn, the transition from regular specter to poltergeist practically a physical thing. It always made sense to me why I could feel it. A specter was just a visual representation of a soul. Sure, they could talk to us—or rather, me—but I couldn't feel their touch.

A poltergeist was a whole other animal. They didn't just peek into our world; they were pulled into it. Only grave talkers—and I suppose my father—could see spirits.

Everyone could see a poltergeist.

Everyone could feel them.

And anyone could be hurt by them.

A screaming woman raced for me, blackened foam on her lips like some kind of rabid animal. She stumbled but caught herself, scrambling like a woman possessed right in my direction.

A smart person would move.

A smart person would use their powers against her.

A smart person would haul ass out of there.

Evidently, I was not a smart person.

Instead of getting to my feet, I flipped over and waited. Just as I expected, she dove for me, blackened fingertips reaching for me as her teeth gnashed in my face. But I'd learned my lesson with Agent Greyson. I'd learned that running would just get me hurt.

Running wasn't the answer. Absorbing her soul to get a power boost was.

Her soul fell into me almost instantly, and Miss Abigale Salt had been one horrible human being when she was alive. I gagged as her soul fell into me despite the power of it coursing through my veins, and it was all I could do not to vomit on the grass.

The second pop of a specter turning caught me off guard. Here I was retching on the grass, and, who I could only bet was Mariana, coiled the ghosts into a frenzy.

My mother had faked her own death—twice if I was keeping count—and the glamour she'd used was the worst of the worst. How many people were dead because of her? How many innocents?

It made me sick to think I'd been so sad this afternoon.

I'd been mourning her.

Now, I was going to kill her.

Bishop scooped me up as he volleyed a ball of magic at our attackers, taking the brunt of a spell that exploded against his side—a spell likely meant for me. I found my feet just as quickly as I'd lost them, moving Bishop out of the way as I shielded him with my body.

I wasn't some wilting flower, and I for damn sure wasn't going to let him be hurt because of me.

The buzz of souls sizzled against my flesh as they clanged like a gong in my head. One in particular rose above the rest, the deafening cacophony of him nearly drowning out everything else. It spoke to me, trapped and keening, screaming for help as the giant of a man raced for me. But unlike before, I didn't wait for him to come to me. I dug my feet into the spongy grass before springing at my attacker.

Hands outstretched, I latched onto the hulking poltergeist, his soul clean as the driven snow. Craft Douglas was a small engine mechanic who'd died in the 1980s. He'd been a good father, a good husband, but he'd had a bad heart. He'd left his family too soon and hadn't wanted to leave them behind. Craft wasn't an angry man—had never even been in a fight in school— even though many people made fun of him for being so big.

And my mother had turned him into a monster.

Craft breathed a sigh of relief as he fell into me, but all I could do was feel rage. Rage at what had been stolen from him. Rage that my mother would try to corrupt a good man that way. The sheer power from his soul was enough to do what was needed.

The flash fire of power raced over my skin, coiling like an intangible whip in my hand. And then I wasn't just on my feet. No, I was hovering over the manicured grass. My lent power flashed from my hands, knocking everyone to the ground. Even the woman wearing Katrina's face.

"Come on out and show your real face, Mother," I hissed through gritted teeth. A second ago, I had no idea how I was going to survive this. How I was going to beat her. But now I knew the answer. I had to show the coven that they had a snake in their midst—even if Shiloh had just stood there while we'd gotten slammed. Even if her inaction was a slap in the face.

White-hot energy leaked from me like a busted faucet, and I whipped it at the woman with all I had.

And missed.

One second my prey was in my sights, and the next she was gone like she'd vanished in thin air.

Then, I couldn't think about that anymore. Witches flowed out of the door of the house, many of them holding potion bottles or orbs of magic. But the more concerning thing was the *pop-pop-pop* of souls turning all at the same time. That many specters turning poltergeist at once shook the world, leaving a crack in the ground several feet wide.

That probably would have been bad enough. Except, those poltergeists didn't just remain standing there. As if they'd been programmed to do so, they launched themselves at not just me, but at the witches as well. I caught a belt across the face as two of them attacked me at once, the coppery tang of blood pissing me off. Without hesitation, my glowing white hands latched onto them, yanking them into me, absorbing their souls and sending them on.

I knew I shouldn't be as pissed as I was. Knew I shouldn't blame them for being used this way, but the blind fury in my gut refused to be denied.

The newly solid specters attacked the witches, slashing at them with blackened fingers, gnashing at them with foaming mouths, tossing them with a strength that shouldn't be theirs. The wind whipped as thunder rolled, a lightning bolt hit the ground right next to the house, showering sparks all over the lawn. Some of the embers caught, the addition of fire was now in the mix as we were getting our asses handed to us.

What should have been a simple death notification

turned into an all-out brawl that was going to turn deadly if I didn't help.

Then, like an idiot—*because let's face it, I was*—I called the feral specters to me. In reality, I hadn't exactly expected them to come—and most definitely—not all at once. But because my luck was the shittiest luck in all the land, each one of those motherfuckers descended on me en masse.

And it wasn't like I could run. It wasn't like I could do a damn thing except accept them.

All at once.

Like an idiot.

The burn of each soul hitting me one after the other felt like I was being roasted from the inside out. And even though I could give it away as I'd done so many times before, this was different. When I'd absorbed the power before, I'd been doing it from specters. Not fifty feral poltergeists.

This was too much power, and it was going to burn me alive.

The only thing I could think of to do was call for my father, and pray he got to me in time.

Help me. Please help me. Azrael, please.

10

One would think Death himself would always be reliable. Wasn't the saying something along the lines of Death and taxes being the only things that were certain in this world? It sure as shit didn't feel like it.

My hope that Azrael could swoop in and save me died just as quickly as I was likely going to, the blistering burn of souls eating me up from the inside.

Why, Darby? Why would you do that?

Bishop's voice sounded clear as a bell in my head—over the roar of the wind and agony in my body, over the ringing in my ears from the souls manifesting on this plane, over everything. Slowly, I turned my head, each millimeter a fresh dose of pain as I struggled to breathe through it. I'd given as much away as I could, healing my friends, and even the witches who'd attacked us. Witches I'd thought were on my side just a week ago.

But this was too much power for one person—even someone with my parentage.

Please, Azrael. Please help me.

Bishop's face was a mask of grief as he crawled closer, reaching out his hand like I wouldn't burn him up, too. His eyes—which were usually so dark that they could be confused for black—were a blazing gold, the power I'd offloaded to him, healing a cut on his cheek before my very eyes.

"I'm sorry," I mouthed, the act of pushing air through my lungs too much.

Then I couldn't see him anymore. All I could see was a set of black wings as my father landed, his back to me. Then his wings were gone as he spun, facing me like he'd really enjoy wringing my neck.

I'm sorry. I didn't know what else to do. I swear, I'm not trying to die.

Azrael's expression didn't change one millimeter as he sprang into action. His hands latched onto me, drawing the burn away with a simple touch. But just as soon as I could breathe again, Azrael's hands grew harder, his fingers digging into my skin like steel-tipped arrows. Then it felt like I was being ripped in half as the world around us faded away.

A scream clawed up my throat, but I couldn't let it free. I didn't have enough air in my lungs for that. All I could do was hold it in as blackness surrounded me.

I couldn't say for sure if I passed out, or if I'd just experienced some sort of interdimensional travel that made me blind for a few minutes. When I could see again, Azrael and I were in the middle of a forest.

Trees with trunks bigger than some compact cars I'd seen sprawled in the lush woodland. The babble of a creek nearby gurgled in the silence as my father stared at me like I was a misbehaving toddler. Given the idiocy I'd just pulled, his judgy look was valid, but valid or not, it didn't make me feel any better.

My first instinct was to want to know where we were, and the second was to wonder how he could take me and not my friends. How could he save me and not them, too?

I didn't ask this question aloud, but I had a feeling my brain was loud as shit right now. The question I did ask seemed less... caustic.

"Did they see you?" Given the fact that the Knoxville coven was still under the impression my father was locked away under several hundred tons of mountain rock and water, seeing him out and about could raise some eyebrows.

Azrael's silence was practically deafening as his expression refused to move even an inch.

"Did I forget to say thank you in the middle of all this? Because I really appreciate you not leaving me to explode."

Azrael gnashed his teeth, reminding me of the poltergeists I'd just survived. Though the feral specters were a little less frightening when they did it. At least *they* didn't have fangs.

My father began to pace, his silence growing more and more oppressive the longer it went on. Dad—Killian —used to do this when I'd really fucked up, and I didn't like it anymore when he did it than I did with Azrael now. It was how I learned just what to do to make criminals talk.

But I wasn't a criminal, and I hadn't intended to do anything wrong. Hell, I still didn't know what I had done wrong. I'd gone to the Knoxville coven to make a death notification. I'd been doing the decent thing. It wasn't my fault everything went to hell in a handbasket.

Azrael sighed long and low like he was trying to keep his soul from escaping his body. "What am I going to do with you? Don't you get that you are fragile? Don't you get—at least by now—that you are being targeted? I have enough dead children, Darby. Why are you trying to join their ranks?"

It would have hurt less if he would have slapped me.

"I'm not," I croaked, inexplicable tears welling in my eyes as the stress of the day hit me all at once. Seeing Mariana on her grave and knowing it was because of me. Then finding out it wasn't her and what she'd done to make the illusion so real. Having my friends attack me. Leaving my friends behind. I brushed my tears away, shoving the pain of it all down deep where it couldn't hurt anymore.

Finding my feet was easy then, the internal buzzing of souls telling me where a large cluster of people were. I yanked my phone from my pocket only to realize it was fried. Pivoting on my heel, I began to head for those souls. Maybe I could find a good Samaritan with a phone. Maybe I could call Bishop or J or someone.

If they're still alive.

"You take too many risks," he insisted, making me turn back.

Easy for him to say. He wasn't the one losing anything.

"Did you know she killed a baby for that glamour? Maybe more? Did you know everything she's done?" Azrael's face was just as blank as it had been before, telling me nothing. Then something dawned on me that I probably should have realized before now.

Some detective I was.

"Is she in league with him?"

My father didn't even blink, but I knew the answer, anyway. The betrayal of it was so heavy I could barely breathe. I hadn't thought it would hurt that much—being betrayed by Mariana—but it did. It hurt worse than being burned up from the inside.

"Did you know the whole time?"

This time Azrael did blink, and as he did, a lone tear raced down his cheek as his jaw clenched.

I'd thought I'd shoved every hurt down, but my efforts were ineffective. Gritting my teeth, I turned back, willing myself not to shed one single tear for either of my birth parents. The best thing Mariana could have ever done for me was leave me with Killian Adler, and as far as I was concerned, I didn't have birth parents.

I welcomed the numbness that those betrayals wrought.

Anytime now. Annnnytime now, it will come and take over, and I won't feel like a piece of garbage.

This was so much worse than Killian keeping the truth from me. Killian had no idea what my mother was capable of, hadn't known the damage she could cause. Azrael did. Azrael knew everything, and still, he put my life in danger.

Tiny puffs of dirt kicked up with each step as I followed a trail toward the buzzing souls. My friends would be okay—Bishop would be okay. They had to be.

A gentle hand slowed my progress, pulling me to a stop. I didn't bother turning to look at him this time. What was his face going to tell me that I didn't already know?

That he was sorry? I knew that already.

That he had to keep the secret? I knew that, too. He made his respect of those bullshit cosmic rules perfectly clear.

That he hadn't meant to hurt me? That might have been so, but it didn't matter.

Not to me.

"If you want to win against them, you will need to find your sister," he said, his voice breaking as he said this. "I'm sorry I hurt you. I'm sorry that I broke your trust. Just know that I am trying to fix it."

I didn't know how a mess of this magnitude could be fixed, but I nodded anyway so he knew I'd heard him. Then his hand was gone, and I was alone to traverse the forest in the dead of night by myself.

Yippee.

I had a lot of time to think as I made my way through the trees in the dark, and I'd realized a few things. One: I was a city girl through and through. Fuck forests and trees and bugs. Just fuck all of it. It was one thing to experience a cabin in the woods with shelter, but hauling my tired ass through this shit in the dark without so much as a flashlight?

No. Fuck, no.

Two: my parents sucked so much I was happy I was adopted. Mariana was a certified psychopath with possible delusions of grandeur, and Azrael's apathy had allowed his children to get slaughtered. She'd turned her back on her team, was working with my crackpot of a brother, and my father was an abandoning asshole with the moral compass of a walnut.

Yep. Happy to be adopted.

Three: if any one of my friends got hurt, I was going to rain Hell down on them like the holy fucking ghost. Naturally, just as I thought this little tidbit, my foot snagged on a tree root, and I face-planted in the goddamn dirt.

Fuck this fucking forest.

Spitting out gritty dirt and who knew what else, I staggered to standing and reoriented myself, heading in the direction of the buzzing souls. It couldn't be too much farther. Right?

About a mile later—*it could have been five for all I knew* —I stumbled across a paved road, the discovery making me practically weep. I seriously considered dropping a kiss to the asphalt but refrained.

Barely.

I could say one thing for this damn forest, and it was that it bore very little in the way of ghosts. Maybe if I gave up my job, moved out to the wilderness, became a hermit of some kind, I could live in relative peace. Just abandon all my responsibilities, throw up a double middle-finger salute, and peace the fuck out. Would X really come looking for me all the way out in the woods if I wasn't sticking my nose in his shit?

No, but Mariana sure as shit would. She'd find your ass just so she could be a thorn in it.

And I'd also miss Dad. I'd miss J and Jimmy. I'd miss being a cop. I'd miss the thrill of being on the job, solving murders, saving people. Once upon a time, that had all been worth it. After spending nearly a year in an ABI prison, the thrill was gone. Maybe if I could convince a certain death mage to come with me it wouldn't be so bad.

I swallowed down my worry and pointed my feet in the direction of what I assumed was a town. I had no doubt we were still in Tennessee, but where, exactly, was a mystery. I needed to figure out if there was a magic-proof phone case I could get that would prevent my phone from turning into a brick.

Someone in the arcane world had to have thought of one, right?

I felt the souls in the car long before I saw the headlights, practically wilting to the ground once I recognized them. I ran down the slight incline, thanking whatever power out there that had kept them alive.

My Jeep screeched to a halt once the headlights fell over me, but I kept running. The door opened, and Bishop climbed out, winking out of sight only to reappear right in front of me. He caught me in his arms and planted a hard kiss on my lips. I kissed him right back, squeezing him tight as the tears I'd been holding back for hours fell from my eyes.

They were okay. They were okay. They were okay.

Bishop pulled back, peppering my face with kisses as the rest of the car's occupants exited the vehicle. J shoved my man aside and gripped me in a bear hug so tight I thought my ribs were going to crack before he, too, was cast aside.

Jimmy and Sarina swarmed me, but I didn't mind.

I'd take a ton of hugs from the only people to never betray me than a single one from the parents who'd abandoned me.

Sarina drew away, her face half-illuminated by the headlights.

"We need to talk."

11

There was only so much bullshit a woman could take before she snapped. I was on the tipping point of just losing my mind and becoming a recluse. For real this time.

"She's a *what?*" I nearly shrieked, my eyes likely twice the size they normally were.

Sarina had just informed me of what she'd been doing over the last few days, and it was safe to say, I was freaking baffled. The five of us were in a diner, and I was on my second stack of pancakes. J and Jimmy were sipping coffee, Bishop was watching me eat with gusto, and Sarina was playing with the sugar shaker as she waited for me to eat my fill.

It was a known fact that Sugar Baby's Pancake House was the best greasy spoon in all of eastern

Tennessee, and if anyone said any different, well, *them's were fighting words.* The diner was straight out of the seventies, and I didn't give that first shit. The cook was phenomenal, and the service was the best in any restaurant ever.

It had turned out that the forest I'd been traipsing through all damn night was up on Haunted Peak, and wouldn't you know it? The first restaurant we'd come across was this all-night diner. Sugar Baby's was owned by Candace Duvall, the late mayor's sister, and it had been in their family for sixty years. Her cousin Dottie was waiting on us, and even though I was a pariah in most of the town, Dottie loved me.

But being a good tipper didn't mean Dottie was up to me causing a ruckus, and my near shriek earned me a disapproving frown.

I mouthed a "sorry" to Dottie before turning back to Sarina. "She's a what?" I whispered, abandoning my food. "You can't be serious."

"A bona fide bounty hunter and mass murderer," Sarina murmured, still staring at the sugar shaker. "Oh, I'm serious, all right. Though, she has cleaned up the streets quite a bit since she's been active."

I put my hand over hers so she'd look at me. "What do you mean?"

Sarina stopped her fidgeting, staring me dead in the

eyes. "I met her a few months ago around the time of that ghoul attack up in Ascension."

"Yeah, I remember that night," Bishop said, nodding. "Paperwork for days, and the mess?" He shuddered. "It was a nightmare."

"Right? Anyway, she was with this crew who brought in one of the culprits who had a connection with X. But she was super standoffish. Funny thing, though, was what I read off of her."

I shoved a huge bite of pancake in my mouth so I wouldn't snap a bitchy "and?" at her.

"Her energy is remarkably similar to yours. Like, damn near identical save for a very key component that she will need to discuss with you." Sarina held up her hand before I could gripe. "No, I'm not telling you, because first off, that would be a total invasion of her privacy. Second, I don't know if she knows it yet, and me telling you is hella rude. Third, it doesn't make a damn bit of sense to me, so explaining it would be far too much work."

I swallowed my bite. "Fine, but I expect you to guide the conversation like you and I both know you're prone to do so she spills her guts. When the time is right, that is."

Sarina pursed her lips like she was thinking about it. "Deal. Anyway, I knew right off the bat that she was a sibling of yours, and given that I was under the impression you were a one-off, I did some digging. People with abilities like yours have huge ties to death magics, the works. What I found was info on her parents. Her mom was some high-up-there blood mage. Was incredibly famous, created nests out of thin air, cast protections on whole bloodlines, and helped forge the powers that be as they are today. Then one day, she just drops off the map. Goes into hiding."

Just like Mariana did with me. Was she the last of us born?

"Yep. Exactly. And she was the last one found, too. According to vital statistics, Rosalind and Peter Cabot died in a house fire. Sloane, too. Then she turns up a year later as a member of the Night Watch after a bounty was placed on her head. A bounty that was marked 'alive only.' The Night Watch claimed she died, but she's still breathing, so..."

J shifted in his seat, leaning forward. "So who put out the bounty?"

"That's just it, no one knows. It's so buried, even I can't find it, and I can find just about anything. Whoever did it has connections."

Sarina didn't say just how uncomfortable those connections made her, but since the thought of it alone made me want to hurl, well, I could empathize. Add this bullshit to how they made it out of the coven house, and well, today—or rather yesterday, given that it was damn near four in the morning—could just fuck all the way off.

I couldn't help but think that there was no X, no mysterious long-lost brother. Mariana seemed plenty capable of being in two places at the same time, wearing glamours only a Fae could see through, and faking her own death. Who was to say she hadn't made this whole X shit up?

I mean, it was bad enough that my wayward mother had turned a close friend against me, but the whole of the Knoxville coven? I'd saved their lives—more than once—and now I was the bad guy?

"I don't know," Sarina muttered. "I can see the logic behind it, but you didn't see what I saw. Those witches are getting fooled and big time. There are enough coaxing workings going on in that house to choke an elephant. I don't think she's X. I think she might be using his clout, though."

"I still can't believe how we got out of there," J said, giving big lovey doe eyes at Jimmy. "I will be fantasizing about that for the rest of my life."

Jimmy had the good sense to blush. "All I did was shield. It was nothing."

All four of us gave Jimmy the stink-eye. According to Bishop and Sarina, shit went haywire after Azrael zipped me out of there. If those witches had been pissed before, it had nothing on when they learned Azrael was no longer in his prison. They rained down curses and hexes on the two ABI agents like they were trying to kill them until Jimmy swooped in. He not only stopped the curses from hitting them, but he also sealed the witches inside the property until the next sundown.

"I should have noticed the look-away spells on the property. I never should have let you guys go in alone. I mean, we were just standing there while you guys could have died..." The big man shook his head. "I should have known better."

Reaching for him was second nature. I'd been comforting Jimmy Hanson since I was a kid. This wasn't the first time I'd have to tell him just how special he was, but it was the first time I'd have to tell a Fae that I owed them.

"You saved lives today, Jimmy. Not just the people here, but those witches as well. Who knows what they would have done if you hadn't? Who knows what Bishop and Sarina would have had to do?"

Jimmy tilted his head forward so his hair covered his face. "Can we talk about something else, please? Like when you're going to visit this sister of yours?"

Truth be told, I already knew the answer to that question. As soon as I got a shower and a boatload of coffee, I was driving up to Ascension and paying my little sister a visit.

"Are you sure this is a good idea?" I hissed, trying not to vomit on my shoes.

Bishop tilted my chin and dropped a gentle kiss on my lips. "Yes, I'm sure."

"Oh, come on, lass," Hildy muttered in my ear. "She can't be any worse than my side of the family. So what if she's a mass-murdering bounty hunter? Your mother's done worse in two days than this girl has done in a year. At least Sloane's cleaning up murderers and rapists."

Hildy hadn't taken the news that Mariana's toxic reach had grown well, though, he hadn't exactly been surprised. "That girl took a beating and decided to do something about it. Kudos to her. And bounty hunting is better than being a vigilante, right?"

I waggled my hand at him.

"Is he still trying to convince you not to worry about Sloane's past?"

I huffed out a laugh. "Of course he is. Though, given my past and family tree, I shouldn't be so judgy. Still, shade jumping through the ward? Isn't that going to cause some problems?"

Bishop smiled. "Not the way I do it. I've got moves you've never seen, Adler."

It's totally wrong that my whole sex clenched at that statement, right?

"I swear to any deity that's listening, if you two start that shit, I'm going to vomit all over your shoes," Sarina growled, elbowing Bishop in the ribs. "You know damn well I haven't had a girlfriend in over a year, asshole. Stop rubbing it in."

I felt a blush coming on as I surveyed the field around us. It didn't seem right doing this without J and Jimmy, but the two insisted on relieving Hildy's Dad-Watch duties so he could come with me as backup. Personally, I figured they needed the sleep. I knew I did.

"Yeah, yeah. What about Luna in Intel?" Bishop asked, raising his eyebrows.

Sarina shook her head. "Didn't even make it to date number one. She's still engaged and tried to lie about it." She rolled her eyes. "Lying to an oracle. I could never date someone so stupid."

I stifled a snicker, silently agreeing. *Who does that?* "Okay, I'm as ready as I'm going to be. Let's do this."

Without another word, Bishop wrapped an arm around my back and pulled me to him at the same time he latched onto Sarina's arm. Then it was about a millisecond of wanting to hurl before we were on the doorstep of a giant house set far back from the edge of the road. Etched into the dark-blue door was a golden all-seeing eye. Some people called it an evil eye—a ward of protection to scare away bad spirits—but the name varied by culture.

It took a full minute before I got the courage to ring the doorbell. Okay, I didn't get the courage, I was goaded into it, but whatever.

"Are ya gonna stand there all day, lass, or am I going to meet your sister? I'm not getting any younger," my ghostly grandfather sniped.

"You're not getting any older either, jerk," I muttered, but pressed the illuminated button anyway. I waited what seemed like a fucking age before getting impatient and ringing it again.

I thought you said she was home? I shot the unspoken question to Sarina, but before she could answer, the door opened with a flourish.

The woman on the other side of it was white-haired and purple-eyed, vaguely reminding me of Azrael when his glamour shifted. Her cheekbones were sharp, and she was a little shorter than me. But otherwise? I could see myself in the shape of her jaw, in the loose-limbed stance, in the pugnacious twist to her expression.

This was my sister.

"Agents Kenzari and La Roux, right?" she barked, the

words less greeting and more like an accusation. Her voice was husky, as if she weren't quite used to using it, the deeper resonance like mine. She stepped from the house and closed the door behind her, crossing her arms as she faced us. "How can I help you?"

"Sloane? Is your name Sloane?" I croaked, trying not to let any trace of tears well in my eyes. I didn't know her from Eve. She could be evil incarnate for all I knew. But even though my brain was screaming at me to play it cool, my heart was beating out of my chest, and I wanted to hug the shit out of her.

Get it together, Darby.

"Maybe. And you are?" Sloane's face was three steps past wary. Hell, she looked like she was ready to race back inside the door and never open it again.

"My name is Darby, and I think you're my sister."

12

I doubted Sloane's expression would have looked more surprised if I slapped her in the face with a brick, though her nod was slightly comforting.

"Got to say, I wasn't expecting you to just show up here. In fact, I wasn't expecting anyone to show up here. No offense, but the last time people made an unannounced visit, it turned into a bloodbath." She paused, grimacing. "And that was yesterday."

"Oh, I like her," Hildy announced, and at the sound of his voice—or at least I thought it was at the sound of his voice—Sloane startled.

She quickly found him, staring right at Hildy like she could see him, even though he was nearly transparent. Sloane's face got even paler, and she backed up a step, slamming herself into the door.

"Holy shit, can you see Hildy?" Bishop asked, aghast. "Is that a family trait or something?"

I didn't know the answer to that question. I could see him because I was half grave talker, but Azrael could see him just fine, so who knew? I didn't know enough about X to be certain on that front.

Sloane swallowed, her color returning a little. "Hildy?"

The man in question moved closer. "Hildenbrand O'Shea. I'm Darby's grandfather. You can call me Hildy if you like. I kind of like that you can see me. It makes practical jokes a lot more fun."

Sloane let out a little bleat of laughter before shifting her gaze to me. "You can see him, too?"

"Yeah, I can see him all right. But not just him. I see all ghosts. It's why I make a good homicide detective. It's easier to solve murders with a little help from the inside."

"Well, since no one has screamed the house down that you're not allowed to be here, I figure it's probably cool to let you in. We're a weird bunch, but it's home, you know?"

Bishop winced. "Yeah, about that. I *may* have knocked out your comms for a little bit. Didn't want anyone flambéing us before we even got an introduction. I'll remove my spell in just a second, promise."

"Ohh, Harper is going to kill you." Then she grimaced. "Not really. I know threatening an ABI agent is probably frowned upon. Just..." She shook her head. "Come on in."

As soon as Sloane opened the door, a white *something* streaked out of the entrance and right into my arms. Then I was staring at glowing green eyes as I held onto what looked like a skeleton cat. Now, this wasn't the first psychopomp I'd ever seen, but that didn't mean I was cool with a reanimated feline just chilling in my arms.

Though, that thought changed when the thing started purring and rubbing her kitty head against my jaw.

"Umm... that's Isis," Sloane muttered, staring at the cat with a teensy hint of betrayal. "I thought I was the only one she did that to. Must be Daddy's death juice."

It took everything in me not to do a full body shudder. "Death juice? Eww, that's just wrong." I stifled a gag as she ushered us into the house. "I do not need to think about our father's sperm, thank you."

Sloane pivoted on a heel and gave the most incredulous stare I'd ever seen.

"Okay, so maybe we'll get along just fine." She then dissolved into a snickering mess, nearly bending double as her giggles turned into full-out laughter. She wiped tears from her eyes as she guided us into an opulent living room.

The inside of the house seemed even more ritzy than the outside, and this was saying something. Gorgeous hardwood floors and plush furniture with bookcases in literally every nook and cranny. I wanted to curl up on one of those couches and read for days. A massive staircase held a giant eagle statue, the wings wide as if it were warding off intruders. But even that couldn't draw my eye away from the sizable blood stain discoloring the wood at the base of the stairs.

Sloane's gaze fell to that stain and her giggles dried up. This wasn't the first time I'd seen a huge bloodstain at an arcane house. Being on friendly terms with the Dubois nest made that an absolute certainty, but this stain held a weight.

As gently as I could, I set the skeleton kitty down— the thing seemed so fragile, I was afraid I'd break her— and faced my sister. Sloane's expression seemed to be an echo of a grief so deep, there was likely no way to express it. It spoke of trauma and loss and pain. I'd seen survivors with that same look more times than I could count.

That look made me want to hug her. I'd never been a big sister before, but dammit, I wanted to be one now. "You okay?"

Sloane blinked, shaking herself as she pasted a false smile on her face. "Fine. We were attacked yesterday. It was—"

"Who the fuck isn't warded in this house? I swear to Christ himself, ya'll better fix it now before I get angry," an already-angry voice called from the landing, cutting Sloane off. "Honestly. Is it so hard?"

Sloane's pasted smile got a real quality to it as she called up the stairs, "We have guests, Harper. Maybe take the rage down a notch?"

A head peeked over the upstairs railing, surprise widening the eyes in an elfin face before they narrowed in suspicion. "Did you do something to my sensors?"

Bishop gave the tiny, pissed-off woman an unrepentant grin. "Yes, but I'll put them back exactly as they were in just a moment. Care to alert Thomas that we're here?"

"He already knows," a male voice grumbled from behind me, the sound of it making me startle. We all turned to the man—no, not man exactly. Vampire. He rested a shoulder on the doorframe before raking a hand through his black, shoulder-length hair. Pale jade eyes, narrowed on Bishop like he was supremely irritated.

Ruh-roh.

It was weird getting snuck up on. One would think as someone who could feel souls everywhere, that would be an impossibility, but it seemed not. Maybe it was Sloane herself that was causing my gift to go haywire. Her soul seemed bigger than all the rest, the buzzing of it so loud, it drowned out everyone else. In truth, she felt a lot like Azrael, like there was too much power for one body to contain.

Wait a minute. Thomas? Ingrid's Thomas?

I must have said that out loud because the man's lips curved into a smile. "I take it you're Darby Adler. I can't thank you enough for coming to her aid. I hate to think that I would have lost her had you not."

"I didn't do it alone," I muttered, tilting my head in Bishop and Sarina's direction.

"Wait," the tiny angry woman—AKA, Harper—broke in, "you guys are the crew that helped the Dubois nest? You realize keeping them alive is the only reason we're alive today. We were getting our asses kicked before they swooped in."

At Harper's words, my ears started ringing. I'd almost lost my sister yesterday—almost lost my own life yesterday. The sheer magnitude of the last week hit me like a pile of bricks, and I needed to rest my hands on my knees before I passed out. Tears flooded my eyes, the stress of it all just a little too much right then.

Sloane knelt down in front of me, her purple gaze

more than a little concerned. "Hey, it's okay. We're okay."

My chuckle was watery, as I muttered the cold, hard truth. "No, it isn't. It's not okay, and we're not okay. Admitting that isn't weakness, little sister."

Sloane blinked at me, the moniker of "little sister" seeming to surprise her. "It's weird that that felt good, right? I shouldn't like that at all, but I really do."

I couldn't help the smile that bloomed on my face. This was just so fucking wholesome, I could burst. "How do you feel about familial hugs? My dad—the man who raised me—is pretty big on them, and considering he's my only stable parent, I'd like to pass that on."

Passing on faking one's own death or being a lying, stealing, back-stabbing asshole wasn't the trait I wanted stamped onto the world if I could help it.

She shrugged, a sheepish expression pulling at her lips, even though she tried to hide it. "I could go for that."

I wasted no time, attack-hugging her with abandon. I'd almost missed meeting her, almost missed all of this. I should have found her sooner. Maybe… maybe if I had, she wouldn't have been alone so long. Maybe she wouldn't have had to forge a family out of nothing. I squeezed her as tight as I could, the hope blooming in my chest for real this time. I couldn't haul off to some deserted island and leave her to take care of this shit herself.

I couldn't give up. Not on her.

"I know I'm dead and all, but choking me until I pass out is still pretty uncomfortable," Sloane croaked, and I pulled away so fast she nearly stumbled until I latched back onto her shoulders.

"What?" I barked, the shock of her words igniting a flash fire of irrational rage in my gut so fast it was as if she lit the match herself. "Explain. Now."

Yes, I used my cop voice on my sister. No, I'm not sorry.

"I—I thought you knew. I figured Azrael would have told you since he sent you here."

I shook my head. "He didn't. Send us, I mean." I jerked my chin at Sarina. "She found you. She brought me here. Azrael hasn't told me dick. Not even your name before yesterday, and he sure as shit didn't mention that you were... *Dead?* Like really dead or like *un*dead? Because I've never heard of a dead girl just walking around all calm like. I mean, Hildy does it, but..." I whipped my head to my grandfather. "How do you do that, by the way?"

"Who is she talking to?" Thomas asked, and I fought off a blush at my gaffe. I'd kept that part of me under wraps for so long, all it took was having another person like me in my general vicinity to break a lifetime's worth of hang ups. Yikes.

"Her grandfather," Bishop answered for me. "Darby can see and speak to the dead."

"I have a couple of other tricks up my sleeve, too," I muttered.

And one of them is screaming mentally for my father to get his feathery ass down here and cough up some answers. What the fuck, Azrael?

"The night I became this?" Sloane said, breaking through my mental tirade. "I died. Azrael tried to bring me back, but I'd been gone too long, so…" She trailed off, and somehow, I knew what Azrael had done. It was what I feared he'd have done to me, too, had he not been able to get to me in time.

"He gave you a piece of himself. He brought you back the hard way rather than let you rest."

Were you out of your mind? I mentally shouted at my absolute bastard of a father, hoping he could hear me wherever he was in the universe. *She could have been at peace with her family, and you thought it was a good idea to rip her from that so she could help fight in your war for you. I swear, you're getting slapped in the face the next time I see you.*

"Did you know your hands glow a little when you're mad?" Sloane whispered, staring at said glowing hands like they were live snakes just chilling on her shoulders.

I yanked my hands back. "Sorry. I was just mentally berating our sperm donor for being an absolute fuck stick. I'll try to keep my shit under control."

"I like her," Harper called from upstairs. "She can stay, and don't bother with the ward. If she's anything like Sloane, she'd burn through it, anyway."

"Ward?"

Sloane smiled, shaking her head as she dropped an arm around my waist. "Harper's an empath, so emotions are kind of a problem for her. We try to be respectful and ward ourselves, but evidently our lineage is kind of a bitch on that front."

She wasn't lying.

13

Sloane led us up the stairs to a carved wooden door, knocking three times.

This was after we met the diminutive Harper in all her glory. I was five ten and some change on a good day. Sloane was probably about five seven or eight. Harper was five feet at a push. Hell, even Sarina—who had been quiet most of the time for some reason— seemed giant next to the woman.

Harper's first word upon meeting Sarina was "psychic?"

"Oracle," Sarina corrected.

Harper shrugged and held out a hand to shake. "Good to meet you."

This seemed to shock both Sloane and Thomas—and myself, if I was being honest. Harper gave the impression that she was the type to dislike ninety-nine percent of the population on sight, so her instant shine to Sarina was a little shocking. Maybe it was the whole "knowing shit they didn't want to know" aspect of it.

I couldn't imagine feeling everyone's emotions or hearing everyone's thoughts. That would be fucking exhausting.

Sarina took Harper's hand, and the tiny woman sighed, smiling. An expression of peace bloomed on her face, softening her features into true beauty.

"What the fuck, Harper?" Sloane growled, almost reaching to touch her but pulling her hands back at the last second.

Harper's gaze broke with Sarina's, her grin pulling wider. "I should have done this before. Maybe if I would have done it with Celeste, then none of this would have happened."

Sloane planted her fists on her hips. "That is not your fault, and you know it."

"Someone explain what is going on, please," Bishop barked, hovering at Sarina's back like he'd rip her out of Harper's hold at any second.

But it was Sarina of all people who answered. "Harper reads emotions naturally through the ambient air, but when she touches someone, she can read nearly every thought, every emotion, everything, and the longer she touches you, the more she can see. Since I'm sort of like her, it isn't as bad as if she were to read another person. Plus, since I'm in the know about all the things, she only has to read me and not the whole group."

"Yeah, but I can't read the future like you can." Harper interjected. "That would have saved my bacon a time or two."

Sarina shrugged. "It has its moments. None that I'd wish on anyone, though."

"Ain't that the truth," Harper muttered. She shifted her gaze to Bishop. "You turn my shit on again or what? Given the environment, leaving us unprotected isn't exactly a good thing."

"Already done, but do a check to be safe. If you need help beefing up the wards, I'd be happy to lend a hand, too."

Thomas scoffed, his arms folded in a mulish stance. "Sure, we'd love an ABI agent just moseying on through our security system. No problem."

Bishop puffed up in affront. "What makes you think after all these years that I would do a fucked-up thing like that. I thought we were friends."

Thomas' eyes went red as needle-like fangs peeked out from under his lips. "Is that what you'd call it?"

"Okay, gentlemen," Sloane growled, sending a steely-eyed glare at Thomas, "let's keep our cool here."

"Yes," I agreed, elbowing Bishop in the ribs. "Let's. I don't know how you feel about the ABI, but I'm not a fan." I looked at Bishop and Sarina, giving them a sheepish shrug. "No offense. But my mother runs the Knoxville branch, and well... She's dirty. Like up to her eyeballs in bullshit, sent me to prison for almost a year, body-snatching, baby-killing, *dir-ty*. She's in the middle of this shit, and I'll be damned if she tries a fucking thing on you, so..." I shook my head, pinching a brow. "If you need help, I got you. You need backup, I'm down. You need me to bury a body, I know a guy."

Sloane snorted. "His name wouldn't happen to be Gerry, would it?"

I blinked at her. Gerry Abernathy was a human with a bound demon inside him down in Whispering Pines. Poor guy made a deal with the wrong witch and got screwed big time. All he'd wanted was to contact his dead wife. What he hadn't planned on was getting possessed by a demon. Last I'd checked, he ran a cemetery at night, so his demon remained dormant. Gerry being off consecrated ground at night would be a very, very bad thing.

"You know Gerry? How is the old bastard?"

"Cantankerous as ever. I can't believe you know the guy that..." She trailed off, shaking herself. "Never mind."

If she knew Gerry, then she'd either buried some bodies herself or knew someone who did—not that I was judging or anything. I knew Gerry because he owed me his life—not that he likely saw it that way, but whatever. So far, I hadn't used his offer to bury a body for me, but if Mariana kept acting up, I might.

"So, you're a police officer who offers to bury bodies for her little sister? And that doesn't make you dirty, how again?" Thomas asked, his jaw clenched, and his eyes narrowed.

Was he trying to get under my skin, or was he just looking out for his friend? I couldn't say, but to hear Ingrid tell it, Thomas was good at getting the truth out of people.

"Who says the bodies we'd be burying would be human?" I asked, tilting my head to the side. "I don't police the arcane, but if you don't believe me, why don't you call Ingrid or Mags. They'll vouch for me."

"Mags?" Thomas sputtered. "The vampire queen of Knoxville lets you call her *Mags*?"

I waggled my eyebrows at him. "That she does. She owes me. Lots. But that's neither here nor there. Now, weren't we up here to meet someone?"

Sloane shoved through our little group and knocked on the door, the three sharp raps barely complete before the thing swung open. A giant of a man was on the other side, his face like a granite slab of pissed-off as he assessed us before his gaze landed on Sloane.

"What's this, love?" he rumbled, his British accent making the question sound sweet when his whole bearing screamed a teensy step down from rage.

Sloane rolled up on the tips of her toes and pressed a kiss to his lips. "I'll tell you in a minute. This is a story only to be told once. Can you get the gang for me? I promise not to start the tale until you come back?"

He narrowed his eyes at her, but a trace of a smile pulled at the side of his mouth. "As you wish, love." His gaze broke from hers and landed on Sarina and Harper's joined hands and grew to the size of dinner plates. "I take it that's a good sign?"

"I think so," she murmured, and the big man dropped another peck to her lips before weaving through us and turning down the hall.

"That's Bastian. He's… we're… he's mine."

Her face leaked so much joy right then, it was all I could do not to hug her again. Inexplicably, my eyes welled up and I had to quit looking at her for a second.

"You happy?" I asked unnecessarily. I knew she was, but as the newly minted big sister, I had to ask.

"Absolutely."

"Good."

Sloane entered the room—which appeared to be an

office—and gestured for us to follow her. The seating was limited—I, along with Bishop, elected to stand. How I was still standing I had no idea. I hadn't slept in I couldn't remember when, and my internal clock was *not* nocturnal.

A woman sat at the sprawling desk, the air of "boss" surrounding her like a cloak. Reddish-brown hair eerily matched her eyes, the red-cast orbs assessing us like we were naughty students brought before the principal. Her steepled fingers were long and thin, and every twitch in them made me nearly jump out of my skin.

Not a moment later, more people filed into the room. The big man—Bastian, a smaller version of him in a beanie, a slight woman with spectacular braids, a tall man with a cowboy swagger, and a... zombie in a house dress?

Sloane clapped her hands together and everyone's eyes came to her—even mine.

"Okay, everyone, I'd like you to meet Darby Adler. My sister. With her is Agent Bishop La Roux and Sarina Kenzari with the ABI. And there is also a ghost you can't see named Hildy."

The zombie chick piped up. "I can see him," she said, fluttering her fingers in a wave at Hildy. "How's it going, handsome?"

"Holy Jesus, Mary, and Joseph," Hildy said under his breath, his finger hooked in his cravat.

It took all I had in me not to start giggling like a ten-year-old, and I shot a look at Sloane who was having a hard time not doing the same.

"Guys, meet my boss, Emrys Zane," Sloane said, gesturing at the woman behind the desk. "You've met Sebastian Cartwright. This is Simon Cartwright." She pointed to the beanie guy. "Dahlia St. James." Sloane gestured to the small woman with the braids. "Axel Monroe, and Clementine Dumond."

"St. James like Shiloh St. James, the Knoxville coven leader?" I asked the woman who was likely a witch. Why she was with this unit and not her coven, I had no idea. Though, given their current circumstances, she was probably all the better for it.

Whiskey-colored eyes assessed me, my question seeming to be a sore spot. "Not sure. I was an orphan."

"Sorry. That makes me less than keen to ask this next one, but Monroe?"

"Yeah, my daddy is who you think he is," the tall cowboy answered, nodding his head. "Unless the bastard has kicked the bucket yet?" The hope in his tone confirmed my suspicions concerning the Monroe ghoul nest.

Technically, there were two ghoul nests in the

Knoxville area: the Monroe nest and the Arnaud. The Arnaud's were getting squeezed out of this area by the Monroe's, and not peacefully, either.

"Not that I know of, but I don't have an in with them." Well, that wasn't exactly true. Quite a few Arnaud ghouls defected to the Monroe nest, and I had an in with them individually, but relying on that would be a horrible idea.

"Can I ask why you're here? It's not often we have ABI agents traipsing through our home. Are ya here in an official capacity?" Emrys asked, her steepled fingers twitching slightly.

"Absolutely not," Bishop answered. "As far as the ABI is concerned, we're not here, have never been here, and don't know you except in passing because of bounties. As far as anyone knows, we don't know you."

"Is that right?"

Bishop shifted, facing her more fully and putting his back to the rest of the people in the room. It was almost like he was shielding me, but that didn't make sense. Until it did.

"The ABI was breached three days ago. Agents I'd known for years slaughtered. At the same time, there was a prison break. I know my director is involved. She..." Bishop shook his head, not able to continue.

"She's my mother," I finished his sentence. "Mariana

O'Shea is my mother, and she has infiltrated the Knoxville coven. That's not why I'm here, but I figure this is a two-birds-one-stone kind of deal. I came here to meet my sister. My friends are here to ask for your help."

Granted, I hadn't known that at the time, and it kind of stung that this was the real reason he was here, but whatever.

"I kind of figured our father would have sent you, but I guess not." Sloane shrugged. "Hey, speaking of, does the name Essex Drake mean anything to you?"

I couldn't recall a name that preposterous, so I shook my head.

Sloane snorted. "Well hold onto your ass. We have a brother, goes by the name X."

"Oh, I know about him. Bastard murderer with a penchant for killing siblings?" I asked to confirm.

"That's the one. Well, Azrael told me to pass along some information. This X? Well, his real name is Essex."

All that research, all that investigation, and Azrael knew this whole fucking time? I wanted to cry it was so stupid. I turned to Bishop, but something was wrong with his face.

It was guilt and shame and something else all wrapped up in a bullshit bow.

Bishop knew who Essex Drake was.

14

"You're glowing again," Sloane said, and it took everything in me to break my eyes away from Bishop's face and look at her instead.

It wasn't just that he knew the name. No, it was that he knew who the man was, and likely, that he was X. I couldn't say why I thought this, but an integral part of me just *knew* it. The betrayal was so fucking hurtful, all I wanted to do was slap the shit out of him. Right after I shot him a few times.

In the kneecaps, not the chest. Calm down.

"Did Azrael give you any other details?" I croaked, trying desperately not to haul across the room and kick Bishop in the balls.

"No, just that he was sorry he didn't tell you sooner."

I only nodded, because if I did anything else, I was going to cause a scene, and I'd just met these people.

"I know who he is," Bishop murmured, and every eye seemed to find him at once.

"Son, I don't know you," Axel began, his drawl thick as molasses and just as deadly as a rattler, "but I'm gonna need you to be real specific on how you know this man and who he is to you."

Bishop skirted one of the chairs in front of Emrys' desk and plopped onto it. "He's the second in command at headquarters in a position called 'The Overseer.' He's my boss's boss."

My eyes welled with stupid, stupid tears, and I just couldn't stay in that room anymore. I weaved through the assembled crowd, needing to be out of that space, away from Bishop, as fast as my feet would take me. It wasn't just my mother that was corrupt. It was her boss, too. Maybe even Bishop.

How could he keep this from me? Did he know all this time? While I was spinning in a circle, chasing my fucking tail, was he just sitting there laughing at me?

One hot tear raced down my cheek, and it was all I could do not to sob my fucking eyes out. I'd thought Bishop was on my side. *Dammit.* How could he keep this from me?

"Wait," Bishop called at my back, but I only moved faster, racing down the steps and taking them two at a time.

I needed to be out of this house, away from that man. I needed it more than air, more than breath.

Bishop closed a hand around my upper arm, and I spun on him, planting my fist in his solar plexus. He wasn't expecting me to go on the offensive, and he tried and failed to suck in a breath. His fingers loosened, and I spun back around, my feet hitting the blood-soaked landing at the bottom of the steps.

"Darby, wait. I can explain," he croaked, but I didn't stop. I wasn't going to let him lie to my face.

Not this time.

And then it was both arms around me from behind as he lifted me off my feet, the awful pull of him jumping through space and time yanking at my gut. But rather than vomiting on him, the rage boiling over inside of me made me fight instead. As soon as we landed, I shoved my heel into his instep and then kicked my legs out. Using that momentum, I let my feet slam into the ground as I bent, flipping the bastard over my back.

My earlier attack must have prepared him, though, because he rolled out of the hard landing with exceptional grace and came right back for me. Only this time, he used his stupid, idiotic bullshit mojo and had me pinned against a hard wall before I could land another hit. Bishop's long fingers encased my wrists at my sides as he pressed his chest against mine.

Golden eyes speared me with an expression of such… I didn't know what I… I couldn't hit him again. All I could do was keep my tears at bay and pray whatever he was going to do, he made it quick.

"Stop," he huffed, his breathing practically panicked. "I can explain. Please just let me explain."

Mentally, I kicked myself. I'd thought he was—or maybe he could be—my person. I thought we were going to be something to each other. Maybe not love, maybe not something permanent, but…

God, how stupid was I?

"You knew X was your boss. You knew who he was this whole time. Did you get a good laugh out of watching me chase my tail? Huh? Was that it? Did you and Sarina just need that laugh under your belts before he fucking killed me?"

And why did I care about him breaking my stupid, hopeful heart instead of the death that was surely waiting for me? Why did I give more of a shit about that than leaving my father, J, and Jimmy behind? Why was I so fucking stupid? Why did I trust him? I should have just kept to myself. That was always the answer, right? Just staying alone would have put a pin in this crap. I was just fine before.

Why did I let myself have hope? Hope was what got people killed.

"No, that's not right, and you know it." He let my wrists go and cupped my jaw, those golden eyes piercing me where I stood. "I would never do something like that —not just to anyone but especially not to you. I—I figured it out after Greyson. The description he gave, it just triggered something—a memory." He let his head rest against mine. "I needed to be sure. I couldn't let you do something rash and get yourself in trouble if I was wrong. It's already too dangerous."

I shook my head slightly, the simple movement making him pull back. "What gave you the right? You could have just as easily told me you weren't sure. That you needed time to prove it first. You know I would have understood." At my accusation, he flinched—just slightly, but I still saw it. "This is more than that."

Bishop sighed before gnashing his teeth together. "The deal you made, when you agreed to the prison sentence, didn't just save my job. It saved my life. My family..." He trailed off, shaking his head. Then he let me go, turning his back to me as he ripped frustrated fingers through his hair. "My family made a deal with the ABI when I was born in exchange for certain protections. I was allowed to live and learn my craft, and in turn, I was sworn to be an agent until I died."

"What? That's barbaric."

Bishop shot a look over his shoulder. "It was five hundred years ago, so it fit the times."

I prayed my face was a blank mask because inside, I was freaking the fuck out. Five hundred years? Five? *Five?*

"Back then, it wasn't just frowned upon for different classes of mages to marry and reproduce, it was against the law. And sometimes, if the marriage wasn't nullified in time, the children were..." He didn't finish that sentence, but he didn't have to.

"So, I saved your life? So what? Like you haven't saved mine?"

Bishop growled under his breath as he turned and marched right back into my space. "Dammit, woman, can't you figure it out? Other than Sarina—who would probably like to shove me off a cliff half the time—you are the only person to give a shit whether I lived or died. I don't know my parents or my family because they gave me away to save their own hides. In five hundred years, no one has sacrificed anything for me. You didn't even like me, and still, you saved my life."

Stupid, stupid tears welled in my eyes. "You brought my father back to me. Of course I made that deal. Anyone would have done the same."

He chuckled, resting his forehead against mine once more. "See, that's where you're wrong," he murmured. "There's no one else who would have done that for me. No one."

"So what? Me saving your ass doesn't quite correlate to you keeping shit from me. Why don't you explain that little nugget?"

"When Ingrid was in trouble—even though you were just healed, even though it was sure to be a bloodbath— what did you do? And when Tabitha was going to absorb all those souls to raise Azrael, wasn't it you that walked in there, nose bleeding, staggering on your feet, damn near dead? When Greyson lost it, who ran right into the fray?"

"I'm a cop, Bishop. It's ingrained in my DNA."

"You know damn well there are hundreds of cops who wouldn't do the same. It's not being a cop. It's you. You do what needs to be done, and I just couldn't risk you doing it this time. Not when I wasn't sure."

I shook my head, ready to lay into him again when he cut me off.

"Don't you get it yet? You are precious to me. I couldn't let you walk into that fray—not with someone like that. Not unless I was stone-cold certain you'd make it out the other side."

"Why?" I didn't mean to ask—*didn't want to ask*—but I did.

Bishop's breath ghosted over my lips in a low chuckle. "There is not a rule I wouldn't break, a line I wouldn't cross for you. I'd rain down Hell itself on this world to keep you safe. Agent or not, I am not a good man. I've done things I knew were wrong for the sake of my own skin. I've killed people for the greater good. I'm not a hero. But I'd burn down the world to be yours."

What could I say to that? There wasn't a response in the world that would do it justice. The only thing I could think of was to press my lips against his. Instantly, he responded, his long-fingered hands cupping my jaw once again. What was it about those fingers touching my face that made me nearly melt into a puddle of goo on the floor?

His tongue swept into my mouth, the taste of him wringing a moan from deep in my chest. I hadn't planned on kissing him, but now that I had, I had no idea how I was going to stop. We had dire, super-important stuff to do, didn't we? Then why couldn't I peel myself from his hard chest? Why couldn't I stop my fingers from exploring the blisteringly hot skin under his T-shirt?

Bishop let my face go and hooked a hand under my thigh, curling my leg over his hip as he yanked me up. And then my legs were around his waist, and we were sitting in a chair? Didn't matter.

Kissing him mattered.

Getting his shirt off so I could taste his skin mattered.

Potentially ripping the rest of his clothes off and burning them in a fire so he had to be naked forever mattered.

The location was irrelevant—especially once the hardness of him pressed against my center. Yup. Totally irrelevant.

Bishop's mouth was at my neck, one hand was tangled in my hair, the other was latched onto my ass, and I didn't know what kind of death mage voodoo he had, but at that moment I didn't care if he bit me, gave me a hickey, or what, because I was T-minus one-point-five seconds from combusting. His fingers tightened in my hair, the bite of it making my eyes roll up into my head as he brought my mouth back down to his.

But he didn't kiss me—no, we shared panting breaths as he stilled my hips. "You deserve better than some old as shit hunting cabin, Adler."

Hunting cabin?

I drew away and finally took stock of the world

around us. Indeed, it was an old hunting cabin, and Bishop was sitting at the small dusty dinette table, in a dingey, rusted-out mid-century chair. The place screamed neglect and abandonment. No one had been in this cabin in decades.

In fact, it seemed like nature was trying to take it back. Vines snaked in the tiny windows, threading through the ceiling joists.

Maybe Bishop had a point.

"You know, until you said something, I didn't even realize where we were. What is this place?"

Bishop gave me his patented naughty schoolboy grin. "It's an old safe house I used about fifty years or so ago. It's seen some better days, but I figured it was somewhere no one would think to look."

"That's real comforting."

He brought a hand up to rub at the back of his neck. "Yeah, not my clearest plan or finest moment. Sorry about that. But it doesn't make it any less true."

And I couldn't blame him. I'd seriously contemplated stealing him away, too. But at least when I planned it, my options were going to include a bed.

"We should get back. Now that you don't want to murder me, that is."

I cackled like a loon. "Who says I don't want to murder you?"

Once again, my body was pressed against his, his hand in my hair, and his lips almost touching mine. My cackle died in my throat.

"Just a hunch, Adler. Just a hunch."

15

I t took us probably another thirty minutes to stop making out after Bishop's "hunch" taunt, and that was only because the chair that we were in collapsed underneath us like a freaking soufflé. Bishop was bleeding, I had a scrape from what was probably a tetanus-infested piece of whatever, and the both of us got the wind knocked out of our lungs.

We gave up after that, heading back to the Night Watch in a swirl of shade jumping bullshit that made me want to die. Sarina seemed to have no problem with it. Why did it damn near kill me every time we did that shit?

After I got my innards calmed down enough to not vomit everywhere, the pair of us approached the property line, the tall grasses giving us a little cover in the wide-open space.

"Tell me why we didn't just pop in the house this time?" I huffed, praying a damn snake didn't decide to eat me. Being from Tennessee, I wasn't exactly a novice when it came to critters, but snakes were not in my wheelhouse.

Bishop threaded his fingers through mine, bringing my hand to his mouth to kiss it. "One: Harper probably beefed up the protection on the property. Two: I want them to know you didn't murder me, and three: it just seems more polite this way. They probably think I'm the damn devil in there."

I could see his point, but the snake factor was still alive and well. My brain had a hard time thinking of the right move. Yes, we knew who Essex Drake was, but getting to him and making him stop was a whole other matter. Plus, I still had no idea why he was doing this shit. Without a motive, I had no idea where to go.

Plus, the title of his job alone sounded ominous as fuck. I mean, *The Overseer*? Just the name alone seemed to explain how he was in all the pies, knew all the dirt, and had a finger on the pulse of everything.

But I didn't have the first clue about how to bring him down... or how Mariana was involved.

Bishop's hold on my hand squeezed painfully tight

before pulling me to a stop altogether. All too quickly, my gaze snagged on the crumpled form in the brush. Snarled dark hair covered half her face, and with her slight stature and fine bones, I pegged her age at about twelve or thirteen at a push. Her face was a mottled mess of bruises, her nose bulbous and slightly off-center, her eyes practically swollen shut. Someone had beaten her, badly.

At that second, I wasn't concerned with whether or not this was a trap, didn't care that someone could have put her in my path to take me out. I flung Bishop's hand off and ran for her. As gently as I could, I gave a cursory assessment. Her breaths were labored like she was breathing through water, her arm was at an odd angle, and her feet... Her feet were fucking hamburger.

The buzz of her soul was so small, so young. Without a thought in my brain, I picked her up, clutching her close to me as I stood.

"Give her to me," Bishop ordered, holding out his hands, and I did as told. As soon as the girl was safely in his arms, he took off running in the dark toward where I hoped a house stood.

I followed at a slightly less frantic pace, but that was only because I didn't want to break my neck in the damn dark like I'd almost done the night prior. Less than an eon later—okay, it was three minutes, but still—we crossed some kind of barrier, the warding of the property barely allowing us entry. I wasted no time racing up the porch and hammering on the door.

The tall cowboy, Axel, answered it, his gaze pulled like a magnet to the girl. "Follow me, and hurry."

We didn't argue as we passed most of the house members and Sarina; we just hauled ass through the house to a secret door hidden in a bookshelf. The dark stone stairway gave off serious dungeon vibes, but I didn't stop, my hand on Bishop's shirt just in case he slipped. The spiral staircase ended in a brightly lit landing that led into a medical bay. Bishop gently laid the girl down and got shooed away by the big man.

Axel pressed a stethoscope to her lungs and instantly hissed. "Dammit all to hell and back. Her lungs are fillin' up. I'm gonna need to operate. Get Thomas in here and Dahlia, too. She smells like witch and hexes and bad shit."

Bishop took off, sprinting up the steps as I did the only thing I could think of, which was to hold her hand. Axel's hands were busy prepping instruments, and all I could think of was helping the girl. The girl's breathing got this wheezing quality to it like the next one might just be her last. The buzz of her life coming to its end clanged like a gong in my head as a sob tore at my throat.

I'd seen a lot of shit as a cop and more as a detective, but I'd only been there at the end, in the aftermath once the dust had settled. And I couldn't think sitting here watching her die was something I'd ever have to do. It didn't matter that she was a complete stranger or not, my heart was breaking.

But I could give her some life, couldn't I? I wasn't sure if I had enough juice to do such a thing, but trying seemed like the only right thing. Wasn't that a saying by someone a hell of a lot smarter than me? When you don't know what to do, just do the next right thing?

Helping this girl was my next right thing.

Closing my eyes to the brightly lit room, I dug deep within myself, locating the spark of a flame that kept me going. The same spark that turned into burning embers when I took too many souls. It felt like it took an age to find that light, but once I found it, I latched onto it as tight as I could, yanking it up to the surface.

"Umm, girlie, I don't know what you're doin', but you're glowing like the damn sun," Axel's drawl broke into my thoughts. "Please tell me I'm not about to have two patients."

Doing my best to ignore him, I willed the light into the girl, praying it was enough.

Cool hands latched onto the tops of my arms. "What are you doing, Darby?"

Bishop.

"Helping," I croaked, waiting to feel her light get stronger. For a second, it didn't. Something was blocking me, stopping me from helping her. But I was a bullheaded bitch of the highest order, and I wasn't going to let this girl die on me—not if I could help it.

Like a dam breaking, the light filled her, and I let it go. Instantly, I felt like I'd been hit by a truck. My body wilted, nearly falling off the chair before strong arms caught me. "See. This right here is why I don't tell you shit. Goddammit, Darby. Tell me you have another bed in this joint."

"I'm just tired," I muttered. "I'm fine."

"Yeah, yeah. Tell that to your bloody nose. I swear to Christ, I'm going to put you in a bubble."

I cracked an eyelid as Bishop started climbing the stairs, the chill of the dungeon or basement or whatever making me shiver. "She was dying. He wouldn't have been able to save her in time. She was too far gone."

Bishop's jaw flexed as he shoved through a door.

"What happened to her?" Sloane and Hildy said at once, and I couldn't help the half-smile that pulled at my lips.

"I'm fine," I insisted. "Just tired is all."

Sloane's laugh was mirthless. "You know I can smell

blood, right? And I have eyes. That hasn't escaped your attention at this point, has it?"

Bishop set me down on a plush couch, and I forced my eyes open to look at my little sister. *Little sister. Man, that was weird.*

"No—though, the blood thing is new. I'll be fine. Faster if you have any ghosts laying around."

"Oh, for fuck's sake," Hildy griped. "This is a damn disgrace. How much of your power did Azrael siphon off of ya, lass? The whole lot? Fucking bastard and his fucking rules. If he had a brain in his head, he'd leave ya with enough to spare, what with you runnin' headlong into danger as ya are." The eyes of Hildy's cane began to glow, the green magic lighting up the skull like a Halloween decoration.

Within a second, I felt better, but I held up a hand.

"Stop. I'm fine. Don't drain yourself too much." I didn't know how much power Hildy had to spare, and losing him would be a blow I likely couldn't recover from.

Probably out of spite, the asshole gave me just a little more. Knowing what I did, I had to figure I was absorbing just a little bit of him every time he did that, and just the thought of it made me sick. Hildy needed to be here, dead or not, ghost or not.

"Quit it. I said I was fine," I ordered, shooting off the

couch. Okay, so it was less shoot and more groaning heave, but whatever.

"Well, at least you're on your feet then," Hildy griped back, his top hat and cane now nowhere to be seen.

"Okay, what the hell was that?" Bastian grumbled, the beefy man crossing his arms as he stared at me like I had a horn coming out of my face or something. "First, you're pissed, running off to who knows where, then you two come back with a damn near dead girl in tow. Then you heal said girl, but that makes you sick, and now you're talking to people who aren't there? Am I getting this right?"

The beanie-wearing guy—Simon, I think his name was—rolled his eyes. "You know what grave talkers are, Bastian. Stop being a twat just because you can't see him."

"For fuck's sake," Hildy muttered before snapping his fingers. In a blink, his hat and cane popped into view, the eyes of the cane glowing bright for a moment. Then Hildy was solid for all the world to see. "Listen to your brother, mage."

Bastian's big arms uncrossed. "Hildenbrand O'Shea, you dead bastard. How have you been?"

Hildy shrugged. "Oh, you know, just trying to keep my granddaughter alive and my daughter from becoming a blight on the family name. You know, the usual."

"You call the most venerated grave talker in the known histories Hildy?" Simon said, aghast. "And he lets you?"

I turned to the man in question. "I'm going to need you to spill on all the grave talker deets. Every time people find out who you are, they freak the fuck out. It's weird."

"All in good time, lass. All in good time."

That means "never" in Hildy-speak.

The sound of the hidden door opening attracted all our gazes. Thomas glided through it, his eyes landing right on me. "I'm going to need you to come with me, please. Alone."

"I don't think so," Bishop countered, pulling me behind him.

Dahlia exited the hidden doorway, her face like thunder. "I want to know what happened to that girl, and I want to know now."

I shook my head. "We found her on our way back, crumpled up in a heap right outside the ward. I don't think I've ever seen her before today."

"Then why is that child saying your name? Why is she calling for you?" Dahlia accused, her face like thunder.

Bishop sighed so hard it was almost a groan, but he finally let my hand go. "No good deed goes unpunished.

Fine. We're all going down there. I won't go in the bay, but I'll be damned if you think I'm letting you take my woman off to some underground lair just so you can accuse her of that bullshit. Not just no, but hell no."

"Works for me," Thomas said, gesturing to the doorway I'd traversed way too many times in the last hour.

And off I went, stepping into the dark.

16

The med bay was tight, filled with far too many people with far too heightened emotions. I could taste them on the air like a coming rainstorm, and I didn't like it. The girl on the hospital bed thrashed and kicked, fighting against restraints far too formidable for such a tiny body.

"Darby! Darby Adler. Detective Darby Adler." That refrain had hastened my steps on the stairs so much I'd almost slipped, and it hadn't quit, even though I'd told her I was there. It wasn't until I'd touched her did the shouts stop, the girl stilling once I laid a hand on her arm.

"I found you," she whispered, her eyelids cracking open just a sliver. A faint smile crested across her face, and I was glad to see her injuries were on the mend. She wouldn't be running any marathons in the near future, but the buzz of her soul was strong enough that I knew she wasn't going anywhere anytime soon.

"You sure did, sweetheart. Can you tell me your name?" I tried not to coo or go into cop mode, both sides of the coin pulling at my brain.

"Poppy," she said, shifting as she tried to sit up. The problem with that was the thick, medical-grade restraints that held her in place. Her dark eyes popped wide as she took them in, yanking her wrists to no avail.

"Shh, it's okay, Poppy. Axel here is going to take them off you in just a moment. You were thrashing pretty hard, and we didn't want you to hurt yourself."

"Get them off me," she pleaded, her tiny voice trembling. "I didn't do anything wrong. Let me go. *Letmego, letmego, letmego.*"

Tears streamed down her face, her still-swollen eyes and nose a testament to just how little I'd been able to heal her.

"Okay, sweetheart. Okay. We're taking them off you right now." I said this as I shot a look at Axel that told him he'd better get his ass in gear before I fucking well made him.

Axel, Dahlia, and Thomas attacked the other restraints as I pulled her wrist out of the closest one. I'd taken courses on trauma and victim's assistance in school, and more of them on my own after I graduated. Normally, it was J who'd do this, though. He would swoop in with his gentle nature and wide smile and put people at ease, while I just made them uncomfortable. But rusty or not, I knew captivity trauma when I saw it.

"There we are, no more restraints." It didn't feel like it was good enough. She'd been confined—I knew that much—and a brightly lit medical bay in the middle of a dungeon wasn't going to be any more comforting than the restraints were. "How do you feel about the sky? Open, fresh air? I think that would do you good, don't you?"

Poppy's gaze skittered around the room, assessing each face before flitting away to the next. Her nod was frantic when her eyes finally landed on me.

"Okay, that's good. Now, my man Bishop is going to carry you up the stairs. Is that okay with you?"

Poppy shook her head as she attempted to scramble back in the bed, only to hiss once her battered feet took a bit of her weight. Her breathing went haywire as her eyes flashed wide, the whites of her eyes damn near all I could see as her pupils went to pinpoints.

Damage control. I need to do damage control.

"That's okay, Poppy. I can carry you. Do you want me to do that instead?"

Poppy shook her head, a frightened keening taking over.

And here comes the shock.

"That's okay, too. We'll just sit here for a minute." I parked my ass on the edge of the bed. "We'll let you get your bearings. No problem."

But pitching my voice low didn't help. Nothing was helping.

"Aww, hell," Axel muttered, pushing me out of the way with his hip as he drew back the plunger of a syringe, filling the thing with what was likely a sedative. "Move." Like a pro, he snagged her flailing leg and swabbed the skin of her thigh with an alcohol packet that he seemed to conjure from thin air. "All right, girlie, I know this is gonna sting, but we need your heart to calm down. This'll help, and when you're feeling better, we'll talk."

Then he stuck her leg, depressing the plunger, even though she was legit fighting him like a freaking wizard. I'd seen combative people get chemically sedated before, but I'd never seen a benzo work that quick. One second, she was fighting, and the next, she was out like a light.

"What the hell did you give her?"

Axel withdrew the needle, and the injection site was covered with a bandage in a blink. What he didn't do was answer me.

"I added a sleep spell to all of the sedatives," Dahlia announced, nearly making me jump. "Normal ones take anywhere from five to ten minutes if they're given in the muscle. This way, we have a non-combative patient whose strength could hurt someone otherwise, and they get to calm down with good dreams."

I thought back to being on patrol for the first year of my career and wishing for something like that. "Have you considered getting a patent? That shit would be like gold in a psych ward."

Bishop snorted. "Do you honestly think we don't have agents in the patent office?"

The implications of the ABI uncovering an arcane drug just out in the wild made me shudder. "Never mind."

The group as a whole moved upstairs while Poppy was still under, and I made it a point to settle her in on the couch with a clear view of the front door. Axel grumbled the whole time, but both Dahlia and I didn't give him another option. The guys went off to do whatever it was that they did, and Sloane, Dahlia, and I sat vigil at the girl's side, waiting for the spelled drug to wear off. For a long time, we sat in silence.

Well, until Dahlia broke it.

Sitting in a leather club chair with her feet tucked under her, she rested her head on her fist and began her inquisition. "Why was she calling for you? It doesn't make any sense. She doesn't know you, right?"

I tried to place Poppy's face in my memories, but as far as I knew, I'd never met her. I wasn't around many children in my line of work, truth be told. "Not that I know of. Axel said she smelled of witch, but sniffing out witches isn't exactly in my wheelhouse, so..."

Dahlia tapped at her lip. "Would it be unethical for me to take a blood sample at this point?"

Sloane rolled her eyes. "From a child? Dude, you know better."

The witch sighed. "Yeah, I do. I just want to know who she is. I feel like I should know her, and I don't, and it's bugging the crap out of me." She pursed her lips in concentration before jumping out of her seat. "I've got it!"

Sloane and I watched as she took off down the stairs, the pair of us blinking at the practical smoke trail she left in her wake.

"I love that girl, but what the fuck?" Sloane muttered.

I had to stifle a snicker, shaking my head. Every witch I'd ever come across was a little weird, but they were typically the kinder species of the arcane. Well, until you pissed them off. Ghouls were of the more barbaric bent, vamps slightly predatory, but witches had a whole live and let live thing going on that I could appreciate.

If only that applied to the Knoxville coven right then.

"You say that your mom is the ABI director here?" Sloane asked, the question coming out of nowhere.

I kept my gaze on Poppy as I answered her with a hand waggle. "Sort of? You know the ABI was attacked a few days ago, right?"

"Of course. We had to round up the fugitives from the prison break. I've never slept so little in my life." Sloane pinched the bridge of her nose. "Then I got blown up. It was a whole mess."

I just blinked at her. "I'm sorry, what?"

"Oh, yeah. So, remember I'm technically dead? Well, I can't exactly die because I'm dead already. So, no worries there, but our brother has—or had—a…" Sloane trailed off like she was trying to think of a reasonable explanation for whatever it was that she had to tell me. "Okay, I don't know exactly who they were to each other. Partner, maybe? Anyway, he had this partner named Celeste who was this gifted syphoner witch, and she did a number on me. She was also basically a Trojan horse kind of deal and damn near got everyone killed, which is why Harper is freaked you breached the system." Sloane winced again. "Actually, full transparency?"

That wasn't her being transparent?

"Uh, yeah?"

"Technically, a few of us did die, but I brought them back?"

I frowned. "What, like a death mage?"

Or like Azrael did for me?

Sloane pooched out her lip and shook her head. "Not exactly?"

"Why are you saying it like a question? Do you not know? Or do you just not want to tell me?"

She winced and blurted, "I went to the In-Between and brought them back."

I let that statement marinate in my brain for a second as I stared at my little sister like she had a hole in her head. Opening my mouth to speak, I promptly closed it again, because what the fuck? How did I just now know there was an In-Between?

At my prolonged silence, Sloane continued, "It's where ghosts live, I think, before they move on. Azrael wasn't exactly forthcoming on the details, but that's what I figure it is. But there's only so much time you can stay there before you get stuck. Simon, Dahlia, and Bastian died, and I…"

"You brought them back," I whispered, sheer awe

hitting me like a brick.

"I sort of got stuck there, too, but Azrael got me back out. That's when he told me to let you know who our brother is. I think he told me because he knew you were coming. And I think he knows something is coming for us. *He* is coming for us. I think Azrael wanted us to be prepared."

That was just the thing, though, wasn't it? Prepared for what? Another attack, another betrayal? "It would be nice if he just fucking told us instead of being so goddamn cryptic. It's tough to gauge what's coming if we don't know the whole story. I mean, given what I've gleaned already, this whole thing is a tangle of vines— only the vines are snakes, and the snakes are venomous."

Light, racing steps sounded before Dahlia emerged with a wad of bloody gauze in her fist.

"What in the—"

"I found some non-creepily sourced blood," she said triumphantly. "I need to find this girl's people—either to return her to her home or beat someone's ass, I don't know which."

The small witch headed for the circular entryway table and hauled the large vase of flowers off of it. In a flash, she had a purple cloth covering it, and at the center was a metal bowl that gleamed in the lamplight.

"What are you doing?" Axel drawled, peeking over the banister as he watched Dahlia assemble her witchy ingredients.

Dahlia shot him a sinister grin. "I'm finding the truth. It's better than eating food, sitting on my ass, or pretending to train."

Sloane, Axel, and I all said an offended "hey" at the same time.

"Don't like my assessment? Fine. But I'm not letting a child just sit here without looking for her people."

At that, she dropped the gauze in the bowl, along with a slew of other ingredients and lit the whole lot on fire with a snap of her fingers. A few seconds later, she extinguished the flames, pouring the smoldering remains on what looked like a map.

Unable to just *sit* there, I got up to see. As soon as the mixture hit the paper, flames ignited, the fire hotter than I'd ever felt in my life. The map burned up, except for three places. Knoxville, a small town in Georgia, and a tiny spec of the map just outside of Ascension.

I studied the three spots that remained of the paper. Knoxville was the base of the St. James witch line. The small town in Georgia was a haven for wayward witches of that same line. And this house had a witch by the same name.

Poppy is a St. James witch.

17

"You're not going to send me back there, are you?" a small voice asked, and I spun to face the frightened child that was no longer sleeping on the couch.

Realizing I must have said my assessment out loud, I immediately shook my head. "If your coven did that to you, absolutely not. I don't give a shit what anyone says."

Immediately, I winced and shot a look at Dahlia. "No offense."

"None taken," she replied, waving my sorry away as she pulled her braids into a knot at the back of her head. "If those bitches hurt you, I promise I'm about to go hurt them."

"Damn straight," Sloane said, echoing the sentiment.

I crossed the room to perch on the edge of the couch by Poppy's covered feet. The blanket Axel had covered her with was one of those super fuzzy ones that felt like a cloud when you ran your hand over it. Poppy was running her fingers over it now in what seemed like an attempt to calm herself, and that action alone made me want to both cry and smash shit.

"Can you tell me what happened?" Honestly, where was J when I needed him? He was so much better at dealing with victims than I was.

Poppy's lip trembled, and I feared the worst until she took a huge breath and seemed to steel herself for the story she was about to tell. She opened her mouth to speak until I heard an intelligible shout from the upstairs landing.

"Wait for us!" Sarina cried as she raced down the stairs with a disgruntled Harper trailing behind her. As our resident psychic and empath, respectively, having them around would be beneficial.

"Oracle," Sarina grumbled. "How many times do I have to say this?" Sarina plopped down on the adjacent love seat, yanking Harper down with her. "Okay, go."

"Stop policing my thoughts, weirdo." Poppy's eyes grew wide at Sarina's antics, and I had to reassure her. "Don't worry about Sarina. She's a sweetheart, promise."

Sarina practically bounced in her seat. "Tell her, kiddo. She'll be pissed, but she's on your side."

Poppy drew back as Harper elbowed Sarina in the ribs. "Quit freaking out the small child, dude. Some oracle you are."

Sloane threw her head back and stared at the ceiling, searching for patience, I guessed.

"It's a madhouse in here, kid. You get used to it. Can you tell me what happened to you?" *I swear to god, if one of you interrupts her again, I will murder you.*

Poppy's tiny fingers reached for my hand, and I freely gave it to her. "I don't know where to start. I don't know... So much of it doesn't make sense. For weeks people have been acting strange. Not behaving like they used to, not doing their normal things, and when I touch the places they have, it doesn't feel like them."

Doesn't feel like them? "I'm sorry, I don't think I understand. What do you mean?"

Poppy rolled her eyes and shook her head. "Sorry. I—I'm a kind of a..."

"In the arcane world, we call you a diviner. It's psychometry," Sarina murmured, likely reading the pictures in Poppy's head. "The word you're looking for. You touch objects and get an impression or a vision off of them, right?"

A diviner? I hadn't heard of one of those before.

"Yeah, that's what Shiloh called it. A diviner."
Poppy's gaze dropped to her fingers again. "She's in
trouble. I tried to get her out, but with her leg, I couldn't
get her to the window."

I sat forward on the cushion. "Who is in trouble?
Where did you come from?"

Poppy's fingers clutched mine tighter. "Shiloh. She
and I were locked in the basement—have been for what
feels like a week. I was asking too many questions, and
this woman locked me up. I'd never seen her before, but
she... hit me, hurt me. I thought when Shiloh saved me,
I wouldn't have to go through that again, but there I was
—only this time was worse. These people were
supposed to be my home—they were supposed to keep
me safe."

Tears tracked down Poppy's face, but she wiped them
off just as fast as they fell. "I need to save Shiloh. The
rest of them can all die for all I care, but she saved me.
Put herself in the way of that woman."

"Son of a bitch," Sarina hissed, her eyes getting that
far-off quality when she was seeing things we couldn't. I
had a feeling I knew who the woman was that Poppy
was talking about, and I'd be willing to bet Sarina
did, too.

"Let me guess, my mother?" I growled, ready to
launch a full-scale rescue mission with the added

purpose of lighting Mariana on fire. But the implications of Poppy's words were just now coming clear. She'd been in the basement for a week.

A week.

Meaning that if Poppy was telling the truth, it hadn't been Shiloh attacking us on her doorstep. It hadn't been Shiloh at the Dubois nest, either. Shiloh didn't kill Agent Easton before I could question him… because she'd been in a basement damn near beaten to death.

And if that hadn't been Shiloh, then who the fuck was it?

Sarina shook herself, blinking rapidly as she came back. Then she stared right into Poppy's eyes and gave her a nod. "The ring, the one you lifted off of her. Give it to Darby."

The child frowned, her left hand pulling back as if she was trying to hide whatever was in her fist.

Sarina raised her eyebrow at the girl, the no-nonsense pull of it scaring even me. "She'll keep it safe. Promise."

Poppy's gaze flitted from Sarina to Harper, then to Sloane before landing on me. "You have to keep it from the man. It's not meant for him. He'll steal it and make it wrong. You have to keep it safe. If you don't…" She trailed off, shaking her head as she kept eye contact with me. "You'll see when you touch it. It's not meant for him, and he shouldn't have it."

"Meant for who?" I asked, though I hadn't meant to say that aloud. I had a feeling I knew who the "who" was, anyway.

Poppy held out her fist, and I opened my hand under it. Once my fingers were in position, she dropped a heavy silver ring in my palm, a large black stone winking at me from the setting. The band was thick with sigils carved in the metal.

Sigils I recognized.

Surrounding the obsidian stone were the same markings I'd drawn on a paper what felt like ages ago—the same ones that had been carved into a dead woman's chest.

This was Azrael's ring—one I'd never seen him wear—but it was his, nonetheless.

What was Mariana doing with Azrael's ring? And what the fuck is going on in that coven?

"None of this makes any sense," I muttered.

"Of course it does," Hildy said, making both Sloane and I jump. He, along with the rest of the boys, had been MIA for the last little bit, so to hear his voice calm as you please startled the shit out of me. "My daughter's used and abused her power and authority as she's always done. She's infiltrated a covens' home, used them and their power for her own gain. She's gone against everythin' I taught her. Everything."

Hildy appeared as if he'd been ravaged, pain etched lines in his face as a silvery tear trailed down his cheek.

It was the "why" that was plaguing me. What could she stand to gain from this? What could be worth killing babies and abusing children? What in her twisted mind would be payment enough for such horrible things?

Poppy saw my confusion—she must have—because she did this odd little head tilt like she was seeing something I simply couldn't. Then she closed her hand over the ring in my palm, latching onto me like she was holding on for dear life.

But it was me that needed to hold on.

One second, I was on that couch in the Night Watch talking to a frightened child, and the next...

I was on a battlefield. Hills and hills of dead men became meat for the crows as I strode through them, their leathers dripping in cooling blood as they fell. So many lives wasted to greed, to hate. The birds feasted as I reaped their souls, sending these foolish mortals to their rest.

The scene changed, and now I was at a fireside.

A woman held her dying son in her arms, the child's fever too much for his tiny body. She pleaded with God to spare the boy, but there was nothing to be done. When he drew his last breath, I cradled him in my arms, carrying him with me as I left her to her grief.

The world swirled before my eyes, and I was once again on a battlefield, only this battle wasn't humans attacking other humans. No, this was something altogether different.

Men stalked the streets with garden tools and torches in their hands, the metal tools sharpened into weapons. They stole through the town, going from house to house as they searched for people not like them. It wasn't a new practice for humans to eradicate things they feared, like a cancer on the earth. They made it to a house I knew well, but I could not intervene. I could not break the rules.

But I should have.

Men dragged her out of her house by her hair, the dark strands now gnarled from their roughness. She kicked and fought, trying to get back to the house, but it wasn't until a flash of bright light made the humans stand back. Fire bloomed over her hands as she scared the humans away, but before she could race into the house, a man emerged from the door with a small, struggling girl in his arms. The child screamed for her mother as she kicked but stilled once a blade was placed against her throat.

The fire in the woman's hands died as she pleaded, but the man only smiled as he slit the child's throat. I held out my hand for the girl to come with me, and she took my hand without question. I drew her into my arms, sparing her witness of what would be done to her mother.

The child was lucky. Her death was quick.

The mother's was not.

The vision swirled again; this time, it was a white-haired man screaming at me.

"You let them die! You just stood there and let those men kill them right in front of you," my son screamed as angry tears raced down his cheeks, his violet eyes—so like my own—flashing with wrath. "You could have saved them, you could have taken those men instead, but you did nothing."

Essex didn't understand, but I did—it was the same as it had always been. A soul only had so much time on this earth—only had so many trips around the sun. I was not in charge of how short or how long the time was.

No matter how much it hurt me.

"You watched as my family died, and you did nothing. I wonder, Father, will you do the same for your own family? Will you watch as they die? Will you sit idly by as they perish one after the other?"

To that, I said nothing. Many of my children had already passed into the Underworld. Never had I spared any of them their fate. "It is not my place to alter fate, son. Only to carry it out."

Essex's lip curled into a sneer. "I make my own fate, and I am no longer your son."

The picture changed again, and this time it was one I knew all too well.

"Tell me, Father, did it look like this?" Essex asked as he held a sharp blade to Isaac's throat, his fingers tangled in my youngest son's hair. "Did my daughter struggle before that bastard slit her throat? Did she cry out?"

Essex didn't want an answer—no one ever really did. No one wanted to know the truth about their loved one's last moments. They didn't want to learn of their fear, of their acceptance that I was coming for them, their regret at the time they wasted. That was too much knowledge for those that remained. Too heavy a weight.

When I didn't answer him, he drew that blade across Isaac's throat like an angry toddler showing his mother he wouldn't be told no. When I didn't react other than to take Isaac's hand, Essex screamed and raved and vowed revenge.

The scenes sped up, cycling through death after death, each one hurting a little more, each one worse than the next. And it wasn't until I got to what appeared like a mass grave did it finally sink in. This was never going to stop. Essex was never going to stop. And not only that, but it had taken Azrael centuries to understand *why* Essex was angry.

Because to Azrael, death was inevitable.

And for Essex, death was the enemy.

The scene changed again, this time, swirling lights

mingled with darkness.

Witches surrounded me as earth and water, air and fire circled me. They meant to put me in a cage, and because I had finally found my heirs, I would go. If I let myself be caged, they could go on unnoticed.

After centuries, I finally understood Essex's rage now— finally comprehended why he hated me so much. Finally grasped the preciousness of a stolen life.

Witches surrounded me—their power magnified by my stolen children. At the center of them was Mariana, the harnessed energy of hundreds of my offspring's souls. How Essex had given them to her, I could not fathom.

The wind shoved me to my knees as fire cooked my flesh, and then she was there, ripping my ring from my finger with a smile on her face. She raised her arms, the water and earth swirling above her as she slipped my ring on her finger.

"For crimes against your children, you are sentenced to an eternity in a box. I hope you enjoy the dark, Azrael. May you rot in it."

Then she brought both of her arms down, and all I saw was blackness.

This time when the scene changed, I realized I was in a different head. Azrael's mind was logical and clinical, almost naïve in a way. But this one was dark and angry, coldly calculating and cruel.

And in that mind, I saw the truth.

18

Hands gripped my upper arms and lifted me off the couch. Warm arms wrapped me up as someone cooed in my ear.

"Breathe, baby. I need you to breathe." *Bishop.*

His rough hands brushed my cheeks, spreading the wetness there as he rocked me in his arms. At his command, I sucked in a breath, the air a sweet kiss to my lungs as they burned from the lack of oxygen.

"There you go, baby. Just keep breathing." His breath hitched, and that one motion had my eyes fighting to open.

It took far too much effort, but I got them open. Bishop let out a sigh of relief once our eyes met, not bothering to hide that he'd been crying. Confused, I brought my hand to his cheek, wiping away the tears.

Why was he crying? Me? That, I understood. But him?

"Wh-what happened?" I croaked, my throat on fire.

Bishop bent and kissed my forehead, a faint tremor radiating through his whole body. "You stopped breathing. Your heart stopped beating. You started crying blood. And then Sarina couldn't hear you anymore. She couldn't see inside your mind. We thought... We tried calling Azrael, but he wouldn't come. God, baby, I thought we'd lost you."

None of this made any sense. Poppy had closed her hand over my fist and then...

Flashes of Azrael's life played like a movie in my head, and then... It took everything in me to not start screaming.

Mariana.

Her plans.

The strength she possessed.

What she wanted to do.

My whole body felt like it had been thrown into a woodchipper, but I still got my poor legs to hold me up as I staggered to my feet, despite Bishop's protests. Hell, everyone's protests. They were all looking at me like they were seeing a ghost.

Ghost. Good one, Darby. Way to be original.

"I need a phone. Now." Yeah, I sounded like a

deranged she-beast, but I needed to make a call and pronto. I didn't really pay attention to who slapped the slim phone into my hand, just that it worked.

I really needed it to work.

I dialed the number I had memorized since the little monster came into my life, and got to experience two rings before a child's voice answered, "This better be who I think it is, or you're going to have hell to pay."

"Ing," I wheezed, my entire body revolting its upright position. "I need to call in my favor."

"About damn time. Jesus. You've held onto the fucking thing for five years." Ingrid Dubois had owed me for far longer than that, but I'd take it. "Is this just my favor or the whole nest, because I gotta say, sweetheart, this week has been a fucking doozy."

I thought about it for half a millisecond. "The whole nest, both boons from Mags, *and* the *three* favors you owe me. And even then, I might have to take out a marker."

The silence on the other end of the line practically echoed. "I will say one thing about you, Adler. You sure as shit are a go big or go home kind of girl."

The memory of Mariana's mind slicing through me made me want to hurl. "It's bad, Ing. Worse than the attack on the nest."

And that wasn't a lie, either. What Mariana had in

store for not just me, but for everyone was three steps past death and far worse than any hell I could come up with. I'd thought my brother was bad. At least he'd had a reason for what he'd done.

Mariana had nothing but greed, nothing but avarice. What she wanted put Tabitha's plan to shame.

"And this is coming for us all?" Ingrid asked, and I looked up from my close inspection of my feet to stare the man I loved in the eyes. I shifted my gaze to my sister, to the family she'd cobbled together, to my newfound friends.

"If I can stop it, no. If I can't..." I didn't bother finishing that sentence. I'd tell her in person what was coming—what Mariana had planned. She'd want that information face-to-face anyway.

"Consider it done. Thomas will tell you where we are. Meet in three hours, yes?"

I nodded, even though she couldn't see me. I didn't know if three hours would be enough time, but I'd take what I could get.

"Three hours," I agreed and ended the call.

Bishop approached, cupping my cheeks in his hands as my knees wobbled. "Tell me. What is it?"

"It's war," I croaked as tears filled my eyes.

It was so much more than war, but how could I tell

them? How could I tell them the worst of it? My gaze landed on Poppy who was curled into herself on the couch.

"Did you see?" I asked, and she shook her head.

"It wasn't meant for me to see. He only wanted the message for you. Said you would know what to do with it. How to stop it." She shuddered, seeming to try shaking the bad thoughts from her brain. "He said that Essex couldn't have the ring. That if he took it, it would bring the end."

But that wasn't the only thing that would bring the end, and somehow, both she and I knew it. She had to know that Mariana's plan was far, far worse than my brother's.

"Azrael," I prompted. "He told you this?"

Poppy nodded.

"Did he say anything else?"

She nodded again, this time her face filled with sorrow. "He said he can't help this time. Not that he doesn't want to, but that he *can't*."

An ice-cold trail of dread filled my belly, making me want to curl up and let the worst take me. But honestly, it didn't surprise me.

Not one bit.

. . .

Bishop was on my ass like Velcro, not even letting me out of his sight so I could change out of my bloody clothes. We didn't have a lot of time to get to the location only Thomas was privy to, so I didn't make too much of a fuss.

Sloane showed me to an opulent teal room, the closet out of either my wildest dreams or worst nightmare, I couldn't decide which. She gave me a pair of leather pants, a spelled tank that she assured me was bulletproof, and a pair of steel-toed boots. I dragged my ass to the bathroom once she made herself scarce, peeling my shirt off as I began to wash my face.

Looking in the mirror, I realized I resembled a damn horror show. Dried blood mingled with fresh, the viscous liquid refusing to release itself from my skin. I scrubbed and scrubbed, but it didn't seem to want to come off, and that was just one thing too many for me. Real tears fell then, the clear saltwater filling my eyes as everything bubbled up to the surface. A sob clawed its way up my throat.

This was too much.

I couldn't do this.

Didn't know how to do this.

Warm arms encircled me from the back as Bishop rumbled soothing words into my ear, "It's going to be okay, Adler. I swear, I'm going to make it okay for you."

A part of me wanted to laugh at the sheer optimism in that statement. The other part just wanted to keep crying. Because I didn't know if we would be anything more than a memory after this. I turned in his arms, throwing mine over his shoulder to wrap him in a hug.

"That's just it. You can't," I admitted, my voice barely above a whisper. "You can't make this right."

"Then tell me what it is, and we'll figure it out. Together."

I pulled back from my hug, my arms barely following my command as I wiped my tears away. "Mariana has a plan of her own. Apart from Essex. He thinks she's working for him, but she's not. She has her own plan. And she needs this ring to do it."

That wasn't all she needed. She also needed me to manipulate the ring for her, needed me to wear the ring as she tore me apart. Needed my soul trapped in the thing for the next part of her plan to work.

"Her plan is to drop the veil, bring down the In-Between, absorb all the spirits stuck there, and..." I couldn't even finish that sentence. Mostly because after what I'd seen, she could not only do it, but her scheme was damn near foolproof.

Bishop's eyes grew wide before his jaw turned to granite. "She wants to kill Death, doesn't she?"

The laugh that broke from my chest was two parts

hysteria to one part sheer disbelief. "I think that is step three of the master plan, yes."

He took a step back, like my words were an actual blow. "Please tell me you're kidding." And then he wasn't just in my space. No, then my ass was against the sink and his fingers were in my hair as he tilted my jaw, so I had no other option but to look him in the eye. "Tell me that you're kidding. Tell me that she doesn't intend to not just kill a god, but—"

"Become one? Yes, that seems to be the plan."

Bishop's left eye twitched as a mask fell over his entire expression. "She means to use you," he whispered like he was reading my mind—like he'd already heard this story and was reciting it word for word. "She can't use Sloane because she's already dead. She can't use Essex because he's too well insulated. But you... You are accessible, alive, and a blood relative. She's going to use you as a conduit so she doesn't burn up."

When I didn't deny any of his assessment, Bishop's eyes got this crazed quality to them as his whole body seemed to tremble. Then he shook his head. "No. No way. You'll die."

"Yeah, I'm pretty sure that's her end goal."

He gritted his teeth. "Then you can't be anywhere near here. You have to—"

"And go where? I have her blood running through my

veins, Bishop. She can find me anywhere. With all the power she's been collecting over the years, storing it in this ring?" I held up the heavy stone to show him. "She isn't going to just want it back. She'll kill to get it. Kill to get me. I have to take the fight to her while I still have the upper hand."

But even that probably wouldn't be enough.

"Can you tell them for me? I need to get dressed and get this blood off," I said, pulling myself out of his arms and turning back to the mirror. I couldn't look at him—not if I planned on doing what I needed to.

"I could turn you, you know," he offered, the words sounding like broken glass falling from his lips. "If… if she needs a living relative, she might not be able to use you then."

It was a scenario I'd contemplated for about a second before dismissing it. I wasn't meant to be a vampire or a ghoul. Hell, I wasn't even meant for this—whatever this was. I was a cop from a semi-small town in the middle of Tennessee who just so happened to see ghosts. It made me good at solving cases—nothing more and nothing less.

"I appreciate the offer, but I'd rather stay me. After you tell them, can you call J? I want him and Jimmy to take my dad somewhere safe. Can you do that for me?"

The silence was a tangible weight around my neck,

but I couldn't look at him, and I couldn't look at myself. All I could do was turn on the water and pray I was doing the right thing.

"Yeah, Adler. I can do that."

19

We arrived at the nest with seconds to spare, the trek taking far longer than I had anticipated, given that Thomas refused to let Bishop just shade jump us in. By my count I was on hour forty of being awake, and I hadn't absorbed a ghost even after damn near dying. The sheer fact that I was still standing was a damn miracle brought on by Clem's otherworldly cooking and a thermos of coffee so strong I was positive it could fuel a space shuttle.

And now I needed to convince an entire nest not to tell me to go jump in a lake somewhere. Piece of cake.

After a too-long trek through dense forest and underbrush, our ragtag crew finally arrived at a cave entrance. There was nothing about the mouth of the cave that seemed out of place. In fact, had Thomas not knocked on the stone three times, I wouldn't have even known it was anything but.

At Thomas' three knocks, parts of the entrance crumbled away only to reform into the shape of a door, the intricately carved wood a thing of beauty. But that beauty didn't detract from the fact that I didn't know where I was, couldn't assess my safety, and was about to ask a bunch of people who owed me their lives to risk them to stop a madwoman.

A madwoman who just so happened to be my mother.

Thomas, Axel, and Emrys entered first, followed by Sloane, Bastian, Simon, and Dahlia. A part of me wished I had Sarina here with me, but she, Harper, and Poppy had stayed behind with the effervescent Clem. It had taken some convincing for both Sarina and Poppy to stay at the Night Watch's house, but someone had to keep watch on the kid, and it couldn't—*shouldn't*—be me.

Staring at the mouth of the nest, I contemplated running just one more time. I could do that. I could run and never stop. A new city every week, a new life. I could be someone else—anyone else. Someone who didn't have a badge, didn't have a family.

Didn't have Bishop.

That was the kicker, wasn't it? There was nowhere he could go that the ABI wouldn't find him. And there was nowhere I could go that would heal the ache of losing him.

Bishop's fingers tangled with mine as I stared at that damn door. I just knew he was thinking the same thing as I was, that bittersweet pill of delusion that said everything was going to be okay. We weren't.

None of this was ever going to be okay.

Bishop chuckled, his fingers squeezing mine again. "Come on, Adler. Don't you want to—"

"Stop." I couldn't take it. Not today. "No jokes, okay? Not right now."

He tugged on my hand, drawing me to him as he wrapped me up in a hug. "They're going to say yes, baby."

He was probably right. Ingrid and Mags would say yes. But then it would be me putting them in harm's way this time, and dammit, I was tired of that. Tired of all of it.

"Oh, would you quit your pity partying?" Hildy griped, and I couldn't help but hide my smile in Bishop's chest as I squeezed him tighter. "Yer actin' like we have time for this shite. Get yer ass in gear and get in there. You're burning daylight, lass."

I chuckled as I pulled away from Bishop, sniffing

back tears and whipping up what I could. "On it, Gramps. On it."

At Hildy's prodding, I stepped into the darkness only to find it wasn't dark at all. What appeared to be a pitch-black cave upon first inspection, morphed into an opulent corridor once I took two steps in. Rough stone walls flattened into polished white marble and the dirt floor to gray slate. Chandeliers dotted the impossibly tall ceilings every fifty feet or so, the metal woven into leaves and vines.

A group of vampires waited for me at the end of the hall—rather impatiently, I might add—until a small blonde broke from the ranks. Racing toward me like I might outrun her somehow, Ingrid used her ancient vamp speed to move faster than I could see. One second, she was fidgeting in the group, and the next, I was wrapped up in a tiny but mighty vamp hug.

Ingrid Dubois was my friend. A *real* friend. I could count on her just like she'd counted on me.

"Hey, Ing," I murmured, bending down to kiss the top of her head. I'd done the same thing to Poppy not three hours ago when I'd emerged fresh-faced from the bathroom. Okay, not fresh-faced exactly. More like puffy eyed from crying and haggard as shit from two straight days of no sleep.

Holding onto my forearms, she pushed away,

inspecting me in the way only she could. Ingrid had lived a few thousand years, and time had taught her a thing or twelve. Reading people was her specialty, and Fates knew what she saw when she read me.

"You don't think you're going to make it," she announced bluntly.

Tell me how you really feel, Ingrid.

"Well, let's take stock," I said, counting off the reasons I was fucking doomed on my fingers. "My mother has been hoarding power for herself since before I was even born. Has an entire coven brainwashed to be at her back, using a mojo that I've never seen before. I've been up for forty hours straight, have no fucking juice, and I'm dealing with a centuries-old diabolical genius who really doesn't give a fuck if I'm her daughter or not."

Ingrid opened her mouth to respond, but I held up a finger because I was still going.

"And my father can't help. So, unless you have a deity in your back pocket that I don't know about, I'm just going to assume I'm fucked and try to figure out a way for everyone else in my life to be *not* fucked if you don't mind. Any theories?"

At my raised brow, Ingrid snorted before she busted out laughing, the childlike laughter coming out of her mouth at a time like this grating on my last nerve. "Way to sell it, Adler. Jesus."

"At least she doesn't beat around the bush," Thomas grumbled, appearing at Ingrid's side like he'd just conjured himself from thin air.

"Better for you to bow out now before we get started than claim I misled you later." If there was one thing I knew for certain about the arcane world was that lying got a girl murdered. Especially when dealing with vampires. Though, if they killed me, it would likely be a hell of a lot less painful than if my mother did it.

"See," Ingrid said, elbowing Thomas in the side. "I told you she was a keeper. Speaking of keepers—"

"I already offered," Bishop said, stopping Ingrid before she pressured me. "She said no."

She rolled her eyes at him. "Of course she would tell you no. No one wants their boyfriend to also be their maker. Plus, she'd be the first of her own line. No protection, no nest, no home. Who the hell would want that?"

"I'm good, Ing." The last damn thing we needed was Ingrid and Bishop going toe-to-toe about whether or not I was changing. "No need to get into a tizzy."

"Tizzy? What are you, a thousand? But for real, though. I'm sure Thomas would change you if you asked nicely." She waggled her eyebrows at me as she said this, likely to annoy the shit out of Bishop.

"Gross," Sloane groaned, hip-checking Ingrid. "That's my sister. Quit making shit weird."

From the lore I'd learned over the years, the transformation process from human to vampire was more than a little sexual. This was why looking at Ingrid sometimes skeeved me the fuck out since she had to have been no older than eight when she'd been changed.

"No thanks, babe. While I'm sure Thomas is a fine gentleman, I have no interest in becoming something other than what I am."

I'd come to the realization some time ago that I'd have a longer-than-human lifespan—or at least I would if my mother refrained from killing me. Add in my father's lineage and what I'd seen from the ring, and I would likely rival Bishop in age someday.

Maybe.

Actually, it was incredibly unlikely that I would live past the night, and it didn't matter one iota what this ring had shown me.

Said ring was currently resting at the base of my thumb, and I wished I had the man who owned it here right then. None of this made any sense. How could the mother I remembered be the same one who put Azrael in a box? How could she be the same woman who brainwashed the Knoxville coven? How could the woman who kissed my boo-boos as a kid be the same woman who would kill a newborn? How could she treat me with so much reverence as a child and hate me so much as an adult?

Right. I knew why, but I couldn't make my brain and my stupid emotions catch up to the facts.

I was slow on the uptake apparently. Forty hours with zero sleep and too much fucking shit to deal with would do that to almost anyone.

But still…

How—as a person with a shred of self-decency—could I be this hurt by a woman who cared so little for me? A woman that subjected me to nearly a year of torture. That threatened me and mine with what she was so eager to dole out?

Why did it hurt so much?

And why did it matter?

Swallowing hard, I steeled myself, and went over my plan with Ingrid.

"That is the dumbest fucking thing I've ever heard of, and I've been around a while," Ingrid growled, her fist in the neck of my top as she drew me down to her eyeline. "You know you're basically signing your own death warrant, right?"

"We don't know that for sure, but this is the only way." Or it was the only way I could think of.

Mariana couldn't get ahold of the power in this ring—not if I wanted my friends and family to stay alive. She could store the power of the souls she'd stolen in the stone, but she could only draw sips from it over time. Regular grave talkers couldn't take several souls at once, their bodies not made to withstand the power. Mariana needed a conduit and she wanted it to be me. But if the ring was empty, she couldn't perform the spell she needed.

I would need to drain the ring before she ever got ahold of it. But I knew what would happen if I did.

"Sloane's already dead—why can't she absorb the souls instead of you?" Ingrid contested, offering a sound objection, but one we'd already debated at length all the way here.

"I don't—" Sloane began, before tears filled her eyes. "I've never taken a good soul. I don't think I can. There are no dark souls in that ring. I can feel it."

Add that to the fact I wouldn't let her do this for me in a million years, and this had been the stalemate we'd come to on the drive here.

"Then why can't Azrael bring his feathery ass down here and take his stupid ring back? Why can't we toss it into a volcano, or make a nice home for it in the deepest, darkest ocean? Have you thought of any of that?" Ingrid griped, and I had to give it to her, she had a point.

But every time I thought about just getting rid of it, I remembered what Poppy said.

Essex can't have the ring. That if he took it, it would bring the end.

I knew without a shadow of a doubt in my mind that if I let that ring leave my possession, we were well and truly fucked. And if I couldn't let it go, and I couldn't give it to Sloane, and I couldn't get rid of it, there was only one thing left.

My small yet ancient friend seemed to only get angrier, her pale eyes turning red as her fangs made themselves known. "It's going to kill you, you know that, right?"

Yeah, I knew that. I knew it, and I couldn't change it —no matter how much I wanted to.

"She knows," Bishop growled, his warm hand finding the small of my back.

Just like I knew that I was going to die, I also knew that Bishop was going to do his damnedest to stop me. Whatever he had to do, whatever sins he needed to put on his soul, he was going to keep me alive.

Even if it killed him.

What a pair we were.

The vibration of my phone ringing in my back pocket

made me jump nearly a foot in the air. I didn't know what sorcery Bishop had done to get me a new phone in the time it took me to get my shit together in the bathroom, but he did it. I'd contemplated calling my dad and J but hadn't quite yet mustered the nerve.

Removing the phone from my back pocket, I quickly realized I didn't recognize the caller. It would just figure that the last person I talked to on the phone was a damn robo-dial. Still, I answered it.

"Darby?" a man hissed down the line, his voice barely above a whisper.

"Yeah?"

He sighed, his breath gusting against the receiver like I was his last hope. "I've been trying to call you all day. It's Owen."

I racked my brain, trying to place him, until I remembered the ghoul I'd saved from certain death about two years ago. He was one of the smaller ghouls I'd met, but a resolute member of the Arnaud line. He'd gotten on the bad side of a pack of shifters, and I'd smoothed things over for him. That was until he'd sided with the Monroe's.

"Owen?"

"It's bad, Darby. The Monroe's are moving against the vamps. Tonight. They—we—sided with the local coven. I-I don't know what to do." He paused, audibly swallowing before he continued. "They have hostages, man. This is bad. So bad."

My gaze found Bishop first before falling to Ingrid. She was listening to the call just like I hoped she would. "It's okay, Owen. You did good calling me. Just tell me what you can."

"I didn't think..." He trailed off, his trembling voice fading away as a sob echoed down the line. "I knew the Monroe's were bad news, but it was join or get killed, right? I thought it would be fine. I should have known better."

I met Axel's eyes, and I knew Owen was telling the truth. Axel had lived it, too.

"They have your dad, Darby. Your partner, too. I got away as soon as I could, but they're expecting me back soon."

The weight of his words knocked the breath out of me, and I had to force air into my lungs.

Breathe in, breathe out. You can do this.

"The witch working with the king said something about a ring. They think you have it."

My chuckle was absolutely mirthless. "Let me guess, they want their lives in exchange?"

Owen audibly gulped. "N-no. Not their lives. I believe she aims to bargain for their souls."

The room spun, and it took everything in me to

remain standing. The best I could do was stare at my Chucks and pray I didn't retch all over them.

"Hey, Owen?" I croaked, trying not to cry.

"Yeah?"

"Next time you see that woman? Can you tell her to go fuck herself for me?"

He stuttered, clearly trying to find a polite way to tell me no.

"Fine. Tell her I'll be there in an hour instead, will you?"

Funny, I'd have thought I would have had more time.

20

What did one do with just an hour to live?

Hug their family? Kiss the man they loved goodbye?

Or did they throw their phone to the ground and stomp on it until it was a gnarled mess of circuitry and shattered glass?

I went with option three, losing the very last bit of my mind as I stomped and smashed and screamed my fucking head off. Hell, if I weren't explicitly trained not to, I would have pulled out my gun and shot the motherfucker. Twice.

Once the phone was reduced to smithereens, I took a deep breath, fixed my ponytail, and met the gazes of every person clustered around me. Some looks were shocked, others full of humor at my antics, but Sloane and Bishop? They knew I didn't have a choice, and their expressions were on the spectrum of ravaged grief. I tried not to feel the sweeping wave of sheer embarrassment or the blind rage that came with it, but both hit me in equal measure.

What was I going to do? Sacrifice the *world* to save my dad and best friend? Sacrifice *them* to protect myself? Let Mariana have her way? There wasn't a good answer or a happy ending.

Not for me, and not for anyone else.

I can't do this, Azrael. Not by myself. Please don't make me make this choice.

Tears leaked from my eyes as I mentally pleaded with my father.

Father. Pfft. What kind of father lets his kids pay for his mistakes? What kind of father allows his daughters to fight his battles for him? You're so hell-bent on following the rules, you'd let the world fall just so you could say you did the right thing.

Well, fuck you, Azrael. Fuck. You.

You should have just let me die in that ravine, you fuck. Why keep me alive if you were just going to abandon me, huh? You're no better than her. I really hope you know that.

"Lass?" Hildy cooed, drawing my watery gaze to him. "You can't go. You can't give her what she wants."

The laugh that came out of me was three steps past hysterical, but it was the only answer I could give him.

"I promise, death isn't so bad. You get to check in on the people you lost. They'll be around you, you know? I doubt either of them will leave you behind." Hildy said this like it was a good thing—like it was an already done deal that I would just let them die to save my own skin.

"So that's where she gets it from," I whispered, staring him right in his eyes. "That's where her absolute disregard for life comes from. Because why would it matter that they were dead? Why would it matter that their lives had been stolen from them? I guess it makes it okay that I could see them, right? Because who gives a fuck if their entire future has been ripped from them as long as it doesn't hurt me, right? Except, your daughter isn't bargaining for their lives. She's bargaining for their souls. To me, that means one of two things. Either she has already killed them and plans on absorbing their souls to power her bullshit, or she fully intends to kill them and make me watch with the last bit tacked on for flavor."

And that didn't even cover what had been done to Jimmy and Uncle Dave. Owen hadn't mentioned them, so it was anyone's guess where they were. They could already be dead. They could be hurt. Something bad had to have happened because there was no way Jimmy would let J just get taken.

Hildy's face went positively ashen—a feat I didn't

think possible on his nearly grayed-out form—but I refused to feel guilty.

Bishop edged into my space, holding out a phone. "Don't smash this one. It's Sarina."

I stared at the thing for a second, not wanting to take it. Phones had done me dirty today, and I wasn't ready for another encounter. But Dad and J were waiting, and time was a luxury I didn't have.

Accepting the stupid device, I held it up to my ear. "Yeah?"

Sarina sniffed, and that one sound nearly brought me to my knees. "They're alive, Darby, and I have a plan. If we stick to it, I think it might just work out."

My eyes found Bishop's, the hope in his sparking just a little in me.

"I'm listening."

The trek back through the forest was a lot easier once the vamps decided to lend a hand. Apparently, me throwing a full-on tantrum was enough to convince them that I needed their help. Considering I'd been nothing but an asset to them since the jump, they were probably going to offer their assistance anyway.

Add in the ghoul problem, and well, it was kind of a no-brainer.

Sarina's plan had about a fifty-fifty shot at actually working. Quite honestly, I figured the odds for a little—okay, a lot—less than that. But her plan was the only one we had that didn't involve me and mine dying slow and painful deaths, so it was our best shot.

"Are you sure this is what you want to do?" Bishop asked, squeezing my hand in his.

We were back in Haunted Peak, back in my hometown. Back to the beginning of all of this shit. I was staring at a cracked bench in a graveyard that had been practically abandoned by the town proper. I'd sat on that bench not even a week ago, trying to fix what Mariana had broken.

I should have known then that this mess wouldn't be fixed.

And am I sure this is what I want to do?

No, I couldn't rightly say it was what I wanted, but I was going to do it anyway.

"Sure. Unless you have a better plan?"

Bishop's dark gaze met mine. "Better than an oracle with a near-perfect track record? I think not."

"Then you have your answer." I moved to take a step forward, and he caught my hand.

"Promise me that when this is all over, it'll still be you and me. Promise me that when we come out the other side of this, we'll go away for a while—just the two of us. We'll just be. No phones, no bullshit. Just us."

I thought of Bishop and me alone at a cabin on a lake somewhere. A place where no one knew us, where we could just be.

A hesitant smile pulled at my lips. "Promise."

"And can you promise to *not* die, too?" Sloane broke in, crossing her arms as she gave me a hard stare. "I can assure you, it's not all that it's cracked up to be."

Bastian threw an arm around her from behind, pulling her back against his front as he kissed her hair. "Easy there, sweetheart."

"Easy, my left ass cheek. She's—" Sloane began, but I cut her off with a hug.

I'd never had a sister before now, and now that I had her, I really hoped I could stick around. "You're pretty awesome, too, you know."

"Yeah, yeah. I'm a damn delight. Just…" She trailed off, squeezing my middle as I rested my chin on her head like any big sister would. "Can you try to stay breathing? I don't have any family left that isn't a raging asshole or a murdering psychopath."

I snorted, squeezing her back. "I'll see what I can do."

With that, I let her go, accepting Bishop's hand once more. This plan had to work. It had to. Turning my back on Sloane and Bastian, on Ingrid and Mags and their contingent, I walked with Bishop toward the cemetery, ready to get this show on the road.

I really hoped Sarina was right—hoped that she didn't see the wrong thing.

"Lass?" Hildy whispered, and I reluctantly gave him my attention. "She's using a glamour—you know that. If I… if I gave you a way to see through it, would that help?"

I thought about it for a split second. "It would."

"I'm sorry for what I said. It was wrong of me to try and see a bright side to this. For what it's worth, I know you're doing the right thing. And… I'm proud of you, Darby. Of the brilliant woman you've become, of the strength you carry. I'm damn proud to call you family."

A second later, the eyes of Hildy's skull cane began to glow. He raised the walking stick so those eyes were level with my own, nearly blinding me with the light. My entire brain seemed to light on fire along with my retinas, the searing ache there and gone in an instant.

"Try that, lass. Should do the trick."

I staggered a bit as I blinked spots out of my vision, the world failing to return to normal. "What the fuck, Hildy? Did you *bibbity, bobbity, boop* me blind? Jesus."

Then the color returned, only it wasn't quite right.

The world appeared to pulse with different hues like I was seeing on an entirely different spectrum of light.

"It won't last more than a day or two, but it should work in a pinch," Hildy said, and I finally got a good look at him. He wasn't a see-through grayed-out specter anymore. No, he was in full technicolor with an aura of darkness around him, hugging his body like a shroud.

My gaze shifted from him to Sloane, and she, too, had the same cloak of death clinging to her, but hers was tempered by peek-a-boo damn near blinding rays of light. It was as if she had a whole sun inside her that was hidden by clouds. I turned to Bishop, relieved to find his aura a vibrant blue, but it was his eyes that were the real showstopper. Instead of just the usual dark brown or the gold of his magic, the darkness of his eyes held a miniature lightning storm complete with rolling clouds and fiery bolts. They were, without a doubt, the most beautiful eyes I'd ever seen.

"I think it's working," I mumbled, letting my new eyes roam over all my friends. "Yeah, definitely working."

Hildy nodded. "I love you, lass, and I'm honored to have watched you grow up. To have a hand in that. You stay safe, you hear?"

Safe wasn't in the cards for me, but I could appreciate the sentiment. "Love you, too, old man."

Then he used his cane once again, making himself solid. With my new eyes, I noticed the difference right away, but I didn't get to really process it because he was now hugging me. I did the only thing I could, hugging him back with all I had. In an instant, Hildy was incorporeal again, and then he winked out of sight.

Probably for the best.

"You ready for this?" I asked Bishop, and if my voice was trembling a little, well, then, so what?

What we were about to do was a level of crazy I had yet to attain. And taking him with me? Sheer stupidity.

"Absolutely not. You?"

"Not even a little." And then I couldn't stop myself from doing the thing that I absolutely should not have done. I turned to him, cupped his face in my hands, and kissed the shit out of him. One long, hot kiss before I broke it. "You know I love you, right? It's stupid, and it's fast and—"

Bishop didn't let me finish. Instead, he banded an arm around my back, yanking me to him. His kiss was molten, exacting. He savored my mouth as he clutched me to him like he'd never let me go. But then he pulled away, leaving me stupefied and dreamy and a hell of a lot less stressed.

"I love you, too, and when you're in there, I want you

to remember that there isn't a rule I won't break for you. Not a single one. So you stay breathing, got it?"

I swallowed, realizing the implication of his words. He'd bring me back, even if that meant death for him. He'd do whatever he had to do.

And so would I.

"That's the plan. Do the same, yeah?"

He gripped my hand in his once again. "Yeah."

Together we walked forward, leaving the safety behind, and stepped into a nightmare.

Two paces into the cemetery, it was as if the world fell away beneath our feet. One second, we were in the Haunted Peak Memorial Cemetery. The next, we were falling through space and time, the landing less than ideal. I felt my ankle give way as my feet made contact with the ground, the bone snapping like a dry twig.

Slapping a hand over my mouth, I barely kept from screaming. But my silence wasn't necessary or required. Hell, as soon as I got a glimpse of the world around me, I wanted to kick Sarina right in her delicate shin. Or maybe punch her in the face. Really, it was dealer's choice.

Because we weren't in the cemetery anymore, and Mariana?

Well, she was looking right at me.

21

A fun fact about the new peepers that Hildy gave me was that I could tell that my she-beast of a mother was wearing a glamour. I could easily see the spell itself, how it clung to her features, how it made her blonde hair dark, her blue eyes brown, her frame taller, thinner.

My mother's body was squatting inside Shiloh's skin like a toad. Her putrid, stained soul clouding the visage of my beautiful friend. I'd been wrong when I'd thought it was Mariana in Katrina's skin. She hadn't been wearing her face at all. She'd been masquerading as Shiloh on and off for at least a week. Maybe longer.

But did it really matter what façade she was wearing?

Not particularly. She couldn't hide behind someone else's face—at least she couldn't right then.

And I tried not to take my eyes off of her for a single second, but I had to see Bishop. Somehow, I'd lost hold of his hand in the fall, and the loss of it made the fucked-up situation all the worse. His soul buzzed at me like a beacon, but he hadn't made a single peep since we'd landed.

I flitted my gaze away from her for just a moment to see Bishop lying motionless, facing away from me, but that's all it took for her to attack. It really did figure that she'd kick me while I was down. That was her modus operandi, after all, and had been for years.

The boot came directly for my ribs, at least two of the bones buckling under the weight of the steel toe. "What? No hello for your mother, Darby?" Mariana taunted in Shiloh's voice. "I'm appalled at your manners."

I didn't have the energy to keep the derision off my face. I was too busy trying to breathe, cursing Sarina in my head, and doing my best not to scream. My fingers clawed at the warm sand, as I wished I had something a bit more substantial to hold onto, doing my best not to howl in agony.

"You are not... my mother... No matter... what skin... you're wearing. Blood doesn't... make you... family," I gasped, struggling to find my way through the pain.

Why, oh, why did it have to be the ribs?

Mariana's fingers found my ponytail, ripping my head back as she smiled at me with Shiloh's mouth. "Oh, I beg to differ. Familial blood is the only reason you're here right now. Did you like your trap? Sarina set it up just for you. *I* figured you'd be too stupid to actually return to town, but here you are just waltzing in here like you own the place."

The woman in question sidled up next to Mariana, a genial smile on her face.

"I really hope you like it. I worked hard on it," Sarina said serenely, like she was a flighty psychic and not the brass knuckles of a woman she really was.

The expression on Sarina's face did not match the twinkle in her eye, but Mariana wasn't looking at her, so it didn't really matter. Plus, Mariana couldn't see what I could. Sarina carried an aura of brilliant stars and swirls like the cosmos, the brightest of whites mingled with the darkest of blues, both colors hugging her like a well-loved child.

It was true that Sarina did have me waltz right into a trap, but since she had explicitly informed me about said trap, well, it was just the matter of the broken bones that I was pissed about. Still, I'd been betrayed a lot over the last little bit, so selling it wasn't too hard.

All I had to do was think of all the times I'd wished

216 | ANNIE ANDERSON

for my mother while growing up. When I tried out for little league football and Coach Williams said I was too skinny and too girly to be on his team. When I got my cycle for the first time and started seeing ghosts. When I had my heart broken. When I went to prom. When I graduated, joined the academy, made detective. She could have been there, but she wasn't.

She could have loved me like a mother should.

But she didn't.

Bitter tears fell from my eyes, cascading down my cheeks as I looked Mariana right in the face. Squirming inside Shiloh's skin, I could really see just how ugly she was, how self-absorbed and selfish. All she'd ever wanted was more power than her father had. Be more adored than her father was. She wanted the fame, the esteem, and the most horrible thing about it was, was that she already had it.

She was an ABI Director for fuck's sake. Wasn't that enough?

Oh, no. She needed to unmake the whole fucking world because her daddy was too famous.

"Fuck... you."

Mariana giggled—she actually fucking *giggled* at me, pressing her hands to her cheeks like I was the most precious little idiot she'd ever seen in her life. Like she had already won. Like she had nothing to fear from me.

At least she let go of my fucking ponytail. The bitch.

"Aww, I think we hurt her feelings," she simpered, and it took all I had not to punch her right in her stupid, smug mouth. "I wonder if you'd like to know all the moves I've made over the years to get you right where you are today."

Would I enjoy hearing a detailed account of her betrayals throughout my life? No. But since I was for sure stalling my ass off, I did what I did best: antagonize the shit out of her.

"Sure. Why not? I figure if you're going to kill me slow and painful, might as well start off with some bullshit monologue." I rolled my eyes for good measure. "Because that doesn't scream super villain or anything."

Mariana tapped her lip like she was trying on the moniker for size in her head. "Super villain. I think I like the sound of that. I wonder if they make plaques with that title on them."

Well, if I had to question as to where my snark came from, I think I found the source.

Despite my better judgment—and the still-broken ribs—I assessed my surroundings. We were exactly where Sarina had said we'd be, a mountain peak with a man-made lake constructed for only one purpose.

To keep Azrael down.

It was funny, the last time I came here of my own

free will, I'd been under the impression I was going to die. Now that it was damn near a certainty, I had a feeling this place had to be bad luck or something. But, hey, I could be wrong.

Monkeys could come flying out of my ass, too.

"I guess if you're planning on killing me, you might as well talk. I mean, going to the grave with unanswered questions just seems cruel. I know that's your life goal and everything, but throw me a bone here."

Mariana scoffed. "I already threw you a bone," she chided, gesturing to Bishop's motionless body behind me. "I knew as soon as he caught sight of you, he'd be on you like a fly on shit. Pity. He really was a good agent, save for the constant complaining." She did a poor imitation of Bishop's deep voice. "'But Director, isn't that unethical? Is this against the law? Why are we doing this?'" She rolled her eyes as she feigned gagging. "It figures he had to have a conscience. It's why I sent him your way. I assumed you two Goody two-shoes would burn up the sheets together. Oh, well."

Mariana's gaze flitted over my shoulder, and I turned to see what she was looking at. A man was walking toward us, tall and lean with a chambray western-style shirt, tight jeans, boots, and an honest-to-god cowboy hat on. I was from Tennessee, sure, but I hadn't seen a man wear a cowboy hat unironically in some time. At first glance, the man had me doing a double take. He looked so much like Axel that I couldn't believe it. This had to be his father, right?

He had the same jaw, same nose. Hell, he even had the same eye color. But this guy was slightly smaller, thinner, and he didn't carry himself with the same swagger. Even in my limited time with the Night Watch's resident ghoul, I still could tell the difference between Axel's confident gait and this man's. Well, that, and Axel's aura was a deep green of a well-fed forest, and this man's was a muddy brown. He was sick, dying, and clinging to life by the skin of his teeth.

Did ghouls get sick? I wasn't sure, but I had a feeling Mariana was out of the loop on that front.

Behind him were four more men, two bound and gagged, their hands tied to thick posts spanning their shoulders.

Both I'd known for as long as I could remember.

Both more precious to me than almost anything on this planet.

Both human and fragile and with no power to speak of.

J sported a blooming black eye and solid gash in his cheek like someone had taken a knife to the inside of his mouth, carving one side up in a macabre smile. And the light surrounding him was gray, mottled with a sickly teal. He'd been hurt and bad—worse than just what I could see. But it was Dad that really had me worried. His face might have been unmarked, but out of the two, he seemed to be worse off. His skin was a chalky white and sweaty, his aura matching J's, all mottled with darkness. He had internal injuries, maybe a bruised liver or kidneys, or possibly something worse. His steps had the bouncy quality of someone barely able to put one foot in front of the other, like each move was a minor miracle of physics.

Trailing behind Dad and J were two more ghouls, the impossibly tall arcaners a head and shoulders taller than their charges. I didn't have that first clue of how to get them out of here, but I *did* have an inkling of just how much this whole plan could go sideways. Sarina's plan was a fragile thing, easily toppled by a single out-of-character choice or misstep.

I just had to pray I didn't make any.

"Ah, Malcolm," Mariana cooed, clapping her hands like a giddy child. "You brought presents."

Malcolm appeared more than a little perturbed at being treated like a lackey, his face bearing a menacing kind of disgust I wished I could duplicate. He held up a fist, and the two henchmen brought their charges to a stop. In tandem, they untied J and Dad, removed the posts from atop their shoulders, and slammed the wood into the sand. Then it was just a matter of retying them. A few seconds later, J and Dad were trussed up like sacrifices, and I was attempting to maneuver my way to standing.

I was failing, but trying all the same.

"I'm done with the song and dance, witch," Malcolm drawled, his Texan accent thicker than Axel's by far. "You either give me what I asked for, or the deal's off."

"What she promise you? Riches? Power? The heart of Knoxville on a platter?" The laugh that escaped my mouth hurt my ribs, but if this Malcom was already half in the bag of hating Mariana, Sarina's plan just might have a shot at working. He only needed a little nudge. "You have to know she doesn't intend on giving you any of it, right?"

I only needed a little opening. One second of them distracted and then I could make my move... after I could stand, of course.

"What's she talking about?" he asked Mariana, and at his question, her face turned to stone.

She gave him a steely-eyed glare. "She's talking out of her ass. And what are you worried about? I get what I want, and you won't have to be concerned with the vampires in Knoxville ever again. That's what you wanted, right?"

I snorted, drawing his gaze. "She means that she'll

get what she wants and kill you afterward, stupid. If there is anything this lady does best, it's distract you with candy while stabbing you in the back." I gestured to the trussed-up hostages, myself, and Bishop. "Duh."

"And what would you know about what I do best?" Mariana hissed, suddenly in my space again, her hand yanking at my hair as she wrenched my head back. Something sharp pressed into the skin of my neck, not piercing, but pretty damn close.

I had just enough hate in me to keep my face placid and voice calm. Just enough rage and patience and spite to not show her even an ounce of the ire bubbling up in my gut. "Why Mother, did I hurt your feelings?"

"Mother?" Malcolm barked, but Mariana didn't take her eyes off of me for a single second.

With her face this close, I didn't even see Shiloh anymore. All I saw was Mariana and the sheer hate fueling her. Unlike Bishop's eyes of thunderstorms and power, Mariana was hatred and greed, putrid poison of a sick soul.

The knife pressed harder against my skin, the bite of my flesh giving way less of a shock than it should have been. It was only a nick, but the promise of her burying that blade in my neck and calling it a day was there.

Her lips curved into the cruelest of smiles.

"Let's get started, shall we?"

22

"Now hold on a minute here. Shiloh St. James doesn't have any children. Who the hell are you?" Malcolm growled, stepping closer to Mariana like an idiot. He should have treated her like a snake about to strike, but that was his fault for not realizing a threat when it was clear as day.

"I said I was leading the Knoxville coven. Who you *assume* I am is of no consequence to me. Now we had a deal. You give me protection so I can complete this spell, and we will make sure the Dubois nest is no longer a problem for you." She didn't remove the knife from my skin or break eye contact, but there was no missing the threat.

If Malcolm didn't fall in line, it would be his throat at the end of her blade, not mine. The problem was that she still hadn't said the words he wanted to hear, and he was about done with her games.

"That doesn't tell me shit, and if you want my help, you'd better start getting real plain with your talk, girl."

She gritted her teeth before admitting a truth I'd only just learned from the ring on my finger. "I am the oldest living St. James witch, meaning no matter what skin I'm in, I have the power. Now they may frown upon mixing of the bloodlines, but they can't deny them, nonetheless. You want the Dubois nest out of your hair, right? Well, give me two hours and they—along with anyone who would oppose you—will be so inundated with their sins, they won't have time to defend themselves against you."

Of all the times for Mariana to be telling the truth. She might have been riding Shiloh's skin, but the blood running in her veins was indeed of the St. James line.

"Look me in the eye and tell me that," Malcolm insisted, and Mariana's gaze broke from mine.

As soon as her eyes were off me, I shifted mine to Sarina. She gave me a slight nod, and I lunged to the side, away from the business end of her knife, drawing my own blade.

I'd only taken one knife-throwing class in my life, and I prayed the lessons had ingrained some sort of muscle memory in that scant amount of time. I let the blade fly, praying it hit something vital. Instead, it went wide, embedding itself in the meat of Mariana's bicep, the knife in her hand falling to the sand.

Malcolm scrambled back, as his ghouls stepped forward, ignoring their charges in favor of keeping their leader safe.

Then it was like everything slowed down.

Sarina took off in a sprint, heading toward one of the cabin mansions as Mariana ripped the blade from her arm. She threw it at Sarina's retreating form, the knife embedding in her back. Sarina's scream was like a punch to the gut as she fell at a snail's pace, her knees hitting the sand first before her torso, and then she stilled.

I was still staring at Sarina's crumpled body, trying to understand. This hadn't been part of the plan. This wasn't supposed to happen. And I was so busy looking at Sarina, I missed my opening.

Mariana sprang at me, her hands like white-hot embers filled with power as they latched onto my shoulders. "Do you think I'm so easily fooled? That I didn't *make* Owen call you? He's dead, by the way. Did you honestly think that I didn't have Sarina figured out weeks ago? That I didn't know about her and Bishop and their snooping? Not likely," she growled as her fingers tightened. She glanced up at Malcolm who was slightly behind his ghouls. "As I *said*, I run the Knoxville coven no matter what skin I'm wearing, and you'd do well to remember that. Now, you will do as instructed, or the next knife will be in your neck."

Without another word to the man, she refocused her efforts on me, snatching the hand with Azrael's ring on it. She began chanting, and that's when I noticed the buzz of souls surrounding us. Mariana's chanting got louder as voices drew nearer, getting closer and closer with each word. The Knoxville coven was out in full force, save for their real leader, and they were backing up Mariana with the full might of a giant coven. Mariana's grip tightened on my shoulder and hand, the heat of not just her hands but the ring itself searing into my flesh.

No, not my flesh. She was forcing the power into me, laundering it through my body like a shady Ponzi scheme. Only this wasn't dirty money, this was hundreds of thousands of souls pouring into me with the force of a whole coven shoving them down my throat. I wanted to offload it, like I'd done many times before, but I couldn't, the working keeping the energy inside me as I scrambled my brain, searching for a way out.

This wasn't the plan.

Sarina said that I was just supposed to stall until they were surrounded. I was supposed to distract her enough that she would miss it when her witches were put out of commission.

Sarina.

I tried to shove the pain aside, tried to hear her, but all I could feel was the fire of souls filling me. All I could do was burn, and scream, and pray someone killed her ass before she tore the world apart.

Mariana's face was practically gleeful as she funneled more and more power into me, her chants growing faster, louder, stronger. I couldn't say what the ghouls were doing, couldn't check on Bishop or my dad or J. I wanted to tell them goodbye, but all I had was the pain of my insides turning molten and the knowledge that I wasn't going to make it. Sarina's prediction wasn't going to come true.

Azrael wasn't going to swoop in and save me. My sister wasn't going to arrive in time. My friends weren't going to make it.

I wasn't going to survive this.

None of us were.

Not this time.

Mariana stopped her chanting, her expression so self-satisfied, I wished for the ability to kill her with my bare hands.

"Do you know why I had you?" she whispered in my ear. "For just this moment. Just so I could do this very thing. Your father, Azrael? He was a means to an end. Just like Killian, just like your stupid, idiotic brother."

I must have appeared confused because she elaborated like I'd mustered the breath for a question.

"What? Do you honestly believe Essex Drake thought all this up? All he wants is revenge for his *poor, unfortunate family*. All he wants is his *daddy* dead. My way, he gets what he wants. They all get what they want." She held my chin in her hand, the grip searing the flesh so much I could smell the cooking meat. I wanted to scream, but even that was out of reach for me. "They want their enemies dead? I aim to please, and they'll never see it coming. Just like they never saw me coming."

Her laugh was like nails on a chalkboard.

"Every spell, every new face, every memory I conjured. You know all the ones of me kissing boo-boos and holding your hand as we played in the backyard? They're all a lie. A fabrication. I put them there to gain your trust. And Killian's that tell him he loved me to distraction? Fake. Tabitha should have learned better under my tutelage. If she had, she would have known to trick you, too. Though, had she learned better, she would have gotten you to keep the souls instead of giving all that power away." She clucked her tongue, shrugging. "No matter. She served her purpose."

Then, she let go of my face, the lack of searing heat almost worse, as the flesh tried and failed to knit itself back together, the power coursing through me begging for any outlet it could find. My ankle and ribs and face might be healing, but the sheer blinding heat inside me was killing everything else. Usually, I'd be a floating *Lite Brite* by now, the power leaking out of me like a sieve, but now it just boiled beneath my skin.

Every noise was too loud, every sensation too much, too bright, too... I could feel souls for miles but couldn't discern them. I could see every facet of Mariana's face, hear her roiling thoughts full of hate and bile, feel every sin on her soul, but I could do nothing about it except writhe in scorching torment.

I knew the instant the ring emptied, turning into nothing more than a gaudy piece of jewelry with my sperm donor's name on it, but Mariana seemed to miss it. She still hadn't realized I'd already drained some of the power before I ever walked through her trap.

But it was never supposed to get this far. I wasn't supposed to take this much. Not one part of this was going to plan, and I wanted to be mad at Sarina, but at this point, I just wanted her to be alive.

I just wanted this burn to go away.

I just wanted my people to stay breathing.

And I wanted Mariana to pay.

Malcolm approached—his soul self-satisfied, even though he was so close to death. He was indeed ill, a magical affliction or a curse of some kind. She must have promised him healing or power or both, and now he was determined to get what he believed he was owed. He crowded Mariana, insistent, but she had no intention of giving him whatever it was he'd asked for.

Silly bastard thinks he can just waltz in here and take? After he barely followed through with his end? I don't think so. Mariana's snide voice was in my head, echoing through my brain like a gong. She was tired, the spell pulling most of her magic, but all she had to do was tap into me and it would all be over for him.

She thinks she's going to stiff me after all we did to back her up? She better pay up or else. Malcolm's thoughts echoed Mariana's, but he had a plan she hadn't thought of—not that I thought it would work.

"You give me what I asked for, and my guys won't slit the throat of every witch they're protecting," he threatened, letting out a sharp whistle.

And that's when all hell broke loose.

One second Malcolm was facing off against Mariana, and the next, a giant of a man was standing behind the ghoul. Appearing from thin air, Jimmy stood in full fighting leathers, sword in hand. I barely registered his battered face or shorn hair or mauled ears. In half a millisecond, Jimmy had his sword through Malcolm's neck. The ghoul's blood sprayed Mariana in a torrent of red as his body shriveled, leaving only his soul behind. Then just as quickly as he appeared, Jimmy disappeared again. Bellows of ghouls calling for their leader echoed through the trees, the screams of witches answering them.

At the sound, Bishop popped up from the sand like a Jack-in-the-box, his feigned injuries catching everyone— even me—by surprise. Raising his hands to the sky, clouds rolled in, darkening everything to pitch as lightning crackled through the air. The boom of thunder rolled through the mountain peak, as bolt after bolt struck, growing closer and closer. Then in the span of a single lightning strike, he had the ghouls guarding my family dispatched, their heads falling to the sand much like their boss's had.

The growl that ripped from Mariana's throat was a thing of beauty, and she reached for me—either to complete the task at hand or to kill me, I didn't know which. But before she could reach me, my throwing knife seemed to embed itself into the meat of her thigh.

The same knife that had been in Sarina's back not a moment ago.

Mariana staggered, shock blooming on her face as Sarina drew another knife from a hidden holster at her ankle.

"Oh, I'm sorry. Did you think you were the only one

who could play dead?" Sarina jeered, letting the blade fly.

Mariana dove to the side, the blade missing her completely. Then she took off, ripping the blade out of her thigh as she ran right at Bishop. Swirls of magic raced up Bishop's arms, but before he could get a shot off, she zagged around him, volleying a blistering bolt of magic his way. It hit him center mass, knocking him off his feet as she made a beeline for her real target.

Jimmy was looking down, untying J's bonds as Mariana sprinted toward them as if she hadn't just been stabbed in the leg. A scream bubbled up my throat as I tried to warn them.

Jimmy glanced up, drawing his sword just a moment too late. Before either of us could react—before we could do a thing to stop her, Mariana threw the blade in her hand, her aim just as true then as it had been before.

As if in slow motion, the knife flew end over end right for my dad.

And then my world fell away as the blade hit home right through his heart.

y father's face was a mask of shock as he stared at the blade protruding from his chest. His chin slowly rose, his eyes unerringly finding mine in the midst of this chaos as blood dribbled from his mouth. I saw the moment he realized he wasn't going to survive—the exact second he knew that the wound was fatal.

I staggered toward him, my feet too slow, my body refusing to let out the power coursing underneath my skin, refusing to help.

I'm so sorry, baby girl. I should have protected you better. Should have done better. His eyelids drooped, his body going slack as his heart fluttered around the knife impaling it, but his thoughts still reached me. *I love you,*

Darby. Will always love you. I'll never regret the extra time I got to spend with you.

His breath hitched, slowed, and still, I was too far away.

My father gave one final gasp just as I reached him, the bitter anguish drowning me as we both crumpled to the sand. For a second everything stopped as I waited for his soul to show itself, waited for him to come to me like Hildy said he would.

But he never came.

Please, Azrael. Please don't make me do this by myself. Please.

But Azrael either didn't hear me or refused to help because he never came.

The scream that bubbled up my throat should have set the world on fire. It should have burned the forest and everyone in it to the ground. Should have turned entire cities to rubble or boiled oceans to nothing.

It should have, but it didn't.

Instead, it unlocked something inside me that I'd never had before: the need for revenge. I pressed a trembling kiss to my father's forehead and then stood, searching for the woman that birthed me with a single-minded focus of a woman over the edge.

I found her in Jimmy's grasp. Mariana struggled against the Viking-like elf, her power now spent after hitting Bishop. A part of my brain wondered if Bishop was okay, if my sister was still alive-ish out there. If her new family was safe and whole.

But the other part of me wanted to burn the world to the ground, and that part was winning. The loss of my dad was a budding flower in my chest yet to bloom, but just the loosened petals had unleashed a wrath I'd never thought I was capable of.

Something inside of me unlocked, as if loss were a key to letting out all the stolen power inside me. I let it flow over my skin, let it form a ball of light in my palm as I stalked toward my struggling mother.

Vaguely, I knew that there was a battle going on around us—understood that my friends were fighting ghouls and witches alike. The buzz of souls clashing—some dying, some victorious—clanged around my brain, but my focus was on the woman wearing my friend's skin, fighting against a Fae's iron hold.

Mariana struggled against Jimmy, her attempts to flee nothing against the rage flowing through him. His thoughts were a jumbled mess of loss, grief, pain, and wrath. Images floated in his mind of the ghouls who'd hurt J, the ones who'd shorn his hair and took knives to his ears. The ones who'd stuck a knife in J's mouth and yanked. The ones who'd beaten my father and Uncle Dave almost to death.

She wasn't getting out of his grasp—not with her head still attached.

I knew the second Mariana realized the ring was empty, her brain abuzz with screeches of disbelief and not a little bit of fear. She'd been so sure her plan would go off without a hitch. So positive that she'd be able to syphon off the power as it burned me up from the inside.

She was supposed to die. Essex said that she would burn up if she took that much power. That lying bastard! He was supposed to be on my side.

"Is that all you care about?" I whispered, enjoying her scrambled thoughts, her distress. "That Essex lied to you? Shouldn't you be worried about what I'm going to do to you?"

Mariana snorted before a patronizing laugh bubbled up her throat. "You won't kill me, Darby." She shook her head, clucking her tongue at me like a naughty child. "I'm your mother. You wouldn't kill your own mother, would you?"

I was positive the smile that distorted my lips was positively feral. "Haven't you heard?" I cooed, malice coating every syllable. "My mother's dead."

Mariana's laugh died a quick death, her smile slipping as she realized I wasn't kidding. There was no such thing as rules right then. No bargaining. There was nothing she could say that would change my mind, no threat she could make.

I didn't care about anything or anyone else. All I wanted was her gone from every plane of existence. I wanted her erased. My gaze shifted to Jimmy's for a moment. He gave me a nod, as he held Mariana still.

"You wanted this power so much?" I asked, nodding at the ball of light in my palm.

Her whole body shook as she ducked her head to shield her eyes from the brightness. "N-no. I don't want it."

"Too bad," I growled through gritted teeth, snatching her chin in my other hand. "You can fucking choke on it." I watched the fear in her eyes mount as I wrenched her jaw open, shoving that ball of light in her mouth.

That light filled her body, but Mariana's was never meant to hold that much at once. It poured from her eyes, her gasping mouth, her skin. That skin cracked like scorched earth, brightness spilling out of the fissures as it ate her up from the inside.

A moment later she was ash and dust as she always should have been.

The relief I thought I would feel never came. All I had now was the incessant buzz of souls in the middle of battle and a rage I couldn't contain.

Might as well make myself useful.

I sprinted away from the water and into the trees where the battle raged on. It didn't matter to them that their leaders were dead, these assholes were hell-bent on destroying everything that had been built just to feed their need for power.

And I was fucking over it.

A giant of a ghoul reached for a petite witch, his catcher's mitt of a hand fisting in the neck of her top and lifting her off the ground. The witch slapped a sparkling orb of a spell into the side of his cheek and the ghoul howled, letting her go.

Another brawl had a ghoul sailing through the air, cracking the base of a tree from the force of the landing. Vampires weaved through the trunks, their blades slicing through body parts like dervishes. Everyone's mind was filled with the battle, with winning, with what they could stand to gain. It all made me sick.

If I'd witnessed this any other day, I probably would have been frightened. Might have been scared at what I could lose. Now, all I wanted to do was make them stop.

And then they did.

Witches and ghouls froze mid-stride, spells burning in their hands, their blades drawn and ready to strike. It was as if I pressed pause on everything, and it was such a relief I seriously contemplated keeping them all like this until the end of time.

"But wouldn't it be boring? The whole world just standing still?" Azrael's voice wasn't the surprise it usually was, so not only did I not jump, I also didn't look at him.

"Can you bring him back?" I asked, not concerned in the slightest at my evident pausing of an entire planet.

"Darby—"

I turned then, the rage for Azrael on par with Mariana. "Don't 'Darby' me. Either you can or you can't. Either you will or you won't. Don't fucking bullshit me, Azrael."

My father stood before me, missing wings, black suit, dark hair, and all—wearing his mask for me like I was some clueless idiot out of the loop. His expression was sad, but for him—what did that even mean? What was sadness when he hadn't given a ripe shit about me my whole life? What the fuck did he have to be sad about?

"I can't, Darby. He's at rest."

Disbelief hit me like a punch to the gut. How could my father be at rest? How could he leave me here alone? How? "That's not fair. He was supposed to live. He was supposed to…"

The ache in my chest brought me to my knees. *He was supposed to live.*

"Killian already passed once. He cannot be brought back again." Azrael tried to say it gently, but his words were like knives in my gut. "He no longer resides in the In-Between. He's gone."

Bullshit. It is all bullshit. Sloane has gone to the In-Between. I can go and bring him back like she did. I can—

"No, Darby. You can't. The In-Between is made for the dead. Sloane might be dead, but you most certainly are not. And she can't go for you because he *is not there.*"

"Then where is he? I'll go get him. Bring him back. I can do that."

Azrael stepped closer to me, reached for me, folding me into his chest. "No, daughter. Killian is at peace. At rest. You would hurt him if you brought him back." He sighed and dropped a kiss to my hair. "I should have told Essex this when he lost his family. I didn't understand then—the loss. I'd looked on from the sidelines since the world began, but it didn't ever make sense to me. Had I been compassionate then—had I known what loss meant—maybe you wouldn't be hurting now."

My breath hitched as tears stung my nose. "You can't fix it, can you?"

Azrael's arms tightened. "No, I cannot."

"Is he—" What was I going to ask? *Is he okay? Is he safe? Does he miss me?*

All those questions seemed trivial and stupid and... I just wanted my dad back. I just wanted my life back. Back the way it was before I started seeing ghosts.

Before I became this tool to wield instead of just a kid. Back when he used to burn the cookies and we'd go to the diner for milkshakes instead. When we would watch old *Perry Mason* episodes and mock his trial rapport. When we were a family of two and happy.

I really wanted that back.

"Yes," Azrael answered. "He is safe and warm and protected. Given the highest honor I could bestow upon him. Because he protected you when I did not—could not. He loved you like you were his own child, raised you with love and care. He made mistakes, but he loved you so much, Darby."

His words weren't the balm he likely hoped they would be, but they did quell my desire to slash through the Underworld like a fucking lunatic.

Barely.

But was I just supposed to keep standing, keep fighting? Was I just supposed to keep breathing?

"Yes. Your work isn't done here."

But I wanted to be done. I wanted to rest, too. Wasn't it my turn by now?

"Your work won't be done for some time, Darby. But you aren't going to be alone. I promise."

With those parting words, Azrael unfurled his wings as he winked out of sight, leaving me to clean up this mess by myself.

I debated heavily on whether or not I wanted to turn the world back on. Pausing it for a while seemed like a really good idea—or at least until I felt less like my heart would fall out of my chest.

But without me telling it to, the world started up on its own, the majority of the combatants falling to their ass. And rather than let them just get back up to start their bullshit all over again, I flexed my unwanted power.

Light bloomed over my hands as I lifted them in the air, the witches and ghouls taking flight as my arms rose. I held them all suspended for a moment before dropping them back to the ground.

"Now that I have your attention," I called, worming my way into their ears. "I would like you to knock this shit off right the fuck now. I'm not going to ask again. Your leaders are dead. I don't want you to follow them, but that's not my choice. You've been misled, tricked into thinking you have the right to take what isn't yours." This was really the issue, wasn't it? Stealing power and territory, hoarding what wasn't theirs to take.

"I'm here to tell you that you're wrong. You don't get to take shit that isn't yours, you don't get to murder without consequence, and you don't get to upset the laws of nature. The Knoxville coven and Monroe nest are both disbanded. I catch you within sniffing distance of

Haunted Peak or Knoxville, and you won't have to worry about the ABI coming for you, I'll dispatch you myself."

I let my gaze drift over shocked- and rage-filled faces, ones full of remorse and ones bent on revenge. I made a note of the rage and revenge people—they'd be coming for me later.

"Lass, what are ya doing?" Hildy asked.

I shot him a look over my shoulder, not letting myself wonder where he'd been for all of this. His face was aghast, but it didn't matter.

Not much did.

"I'm cleaning up a mess."

It turned out that ghouls didn't rightly like taking orders from non-ghoul arcaners. That, and as a rule, they were pack hunters. Four of them ran at me at once, their speed seeming so slow now that I'd absorbed the ring's power.

Without much thought on my part, I raised my hands again, lifting them off their feet at once. With a twist of my wrist, four heads dropped to the ground as their former bodies remained suspended. A moment later, I dropped my hands, their withering husks exploding into dust as they hit the forest floor.

I met the gaze of the closest ghoul still breathing. I knew his name like it had been laser-etched onto my brain. Knew everything about him. He'd been recently turned because of his size, illegally, too. They'd bypassed the covenant and made him against his will. I'd be looking into that sometime later, but for now, he was a threat until he'd proven himself otherwise.

"You want to try your hand?"

Wide-eyed with a healthy dose of fear, he shook his head. "No, ma'am. I like my head right where it is."

"Very good. I know the name of every ghoul here today. Every single one. You run along and tell all your friends that. You have twenty-four hours. One second past that is kill on sight, understand?"

The ghoul nodded vigorously. "Y-yes, ma'am."

"Run along now."

The ghoul hopped up from the ground like he'd been spring-loaded, taking off through the trees. He didn't stop at his nest-mates and gather them. No, he'd taken me at my word, and none of these men were his friends. He was heading back to Knoxville to pack his bags, his plan to make his way back to Texas at the forefront of his mind. Smart.

"I suggest you follow your boy, Lucas' example. You have five seconds to get out of this forest and on out of town." I didn't even get to the count of two before the remaining ghouls were gone.

The witches who'd been left alive after the onslaught were slow to get with the program, the spells turning their minds breaking one by one after Mariana's demise.

Some of their thoughts were jumbled messes of confusion, while others were pissed the plan had failed. Yeah, Mariana hadn't had to spell them all, and the rage of that betrayal burned me up.

At this point, the only Knoxville coven witch I cared about was currently suffering in a basement right then.

"I know your minds. Your names. Your sins," I announced, making sure my voice wasn't just in their ears, but clanging inside their heads. "Your betrayal has been noted. You are not welcome here. Twenty-four hours. Get the *fuck* out of my town. Get your shit out of Knoxville. Out of my state. If I see you, there is no place in this world or the next safe for you."

"Are you sure you want to be doing this, lass?" Hildy asked, but I couldn't look at him again.

"Your daughter set this into motion ages ago—all I'm doing is making me and mine safe."

Hildy got right in my face then, concern stamped all over him. "You're painting a target on your back is what you're doing. Disbanding covens and nests? You realize you're taking the mantle of leader if you do that. Have you thought this through?"

Had I? Absolutely not.

But was I following through? Abso-fucking-lutely.

"If you think I'm going to let this stand, you're out of

your mind. Twenty-four hours is a goddamn gift, and you know it."

Hildy nodded. "In the past, I would have done the same. Gotten revenge. But there are no winners in a game like that. And there's no peace in it, either."

But I wasn't looking for peace. It had never been mine to have anyway.

Grass rustled behind me, but I knew the soul almost as well as my own.

"Darby?" J croaked, his sorrow a mirror of my own.

I watched the last of the witches leave before turning to my best friend. His face was a mangled mess, his body bruised and beaten, but I'd fix that. I reached for him, and he didn't mind the glowing fingers. He just took my hand before falling into me, wrapping me in a hug.

Giving him some of the power roiling under my skin, his injuries sealed shut, his ribs healing, the cut through his lip fading to nothing. His chest heaved under my arms, a sob of grief and remorse and violation ripping up his throat. I wanted to comfort him, I did. But mine had to stay buried until the job was done. Then... then maybe I could let myself feel it. Let myself break.

If I dared.

Jimmy approached, his thoughts muddier than J's. J had been beaten, but Jimmy had been stolen from—he'd been violated in a way that made my heart ache. I didn't know if I could give back what they'd taken, but I could try. I held out my palm for him to take J off my hands, and when he took it, his cuts and mangled ears healed in an instant. In the next, his hair began to grow, falling far past his shoulders and down his back. It was blonder, too, the tresses whiter than anything. Passing the couple, I meandered back to the road, not wanting to see anyone else.

Yes, I needed Bishop and Sarina and Sloane. Needed to see with my own eyes that they were okay, even though their thoughts buzzed like bees in my brain, but I couldn't return to the beach.

I couldn't see my father bloody and broken.

I just didn't have it in me.

Not right then.

I felt the arms before I heard his mind, which given the circumstances, should have made me jump. But Bishop wrapping me in a hug seemed far too good to pass up. Leaning into him, the wall of ice around my heart began to thaw, the bitter ache tunneling through the frost.

Sucking in a huge breath, I tried to power through it, tried to just shove it down, but once it found a crack, it came spilling out of me. I couldn't stop the shuddering sob that fell from my lips or the way my knees buckled.

Bishop eased me to the ground, turning me in his arms as he wrapped me in his.

My dad was gone. *My dad was gone.*

"Shh, baby. We're going to take care of this."

A nice sentiment, but the truth was that there was no taking care of a loss like this.

Not ever.

A soft whine pulled me out of Bishop's embrace and had me gazing down the road. A gray wolf was limping toward us, its fur matted with dirt and dried blood.

No, not *it*. *His.*

His mind called to me, ringing like a gong as he hobbled closer before collapsing on the asphalt.

"Uncle Dave?" I called, scrambling away from Bishop and sprinting down the road.

Bishop tried to catch me, stop me, but I wouldn't be deterred. I nearly slid on loose gravel and fell on my ass, but I got there. Dave panted, his pain echoing through my brain like a cannon blast. He whined long and low, his thoughts on Dad, on what was done to them. In the attack, he'd shifted, but it hadn't been enough. There had been too many ghouls, and he didn't have a pack to go to for backup.

"It's okay, Cap. I've got you." I couldn't tell him the rest. Not yet. Not after all he'd done to get to us.

Laying my hand on his flank, I forced power into

him, healing his leg and his ribs, sealing his cuts. It didn't seem like enough, really. They'd been protecting Dad, and what was I doing? I should have been keeping a better eye on him. I should have…

A mist surrounded Dave before falling away to reveal the man I'd known all my life. My father's best friend. My captain.

"Darby? Did you find Killian? Did you get him?"

All I could do was shake my head as tears welled in my eyes.

No, I hadn't.

It seemed to take forever to get my emotions under lock and key, my crying jag lasting far longer than I ever wanted it to. I had things to do, a witch to save, rogues to catch, etc. I needed to be up and ready for the next wave of bullshit that I knew was coming my way.

If Azrael were to be believed, I wouldn't be resting for a while.

The official story was that Dad had died in a car accident—a bitter pill to swallow since that was the same damn cause of death that had been on my mother's autopsy. Cap convinced Dr. Yates to sign off on the fabricated scene, and I tried not to look too hard into his thoughts on that one to see how he'd done it, either.

While Cap was handling that, Sloane, Bastian, Bishop, and I broke into the Knoxville coven basement to find Shiloh. By the time we got there, the house had been ransacked, bedrooms left empty with drawers half-hanging out of dressers, grimoire pages ripped and torn and littering the hall. But none of them had thought to let their leader out of her cage—probably too scared, I'd bet.

Shiloh had been beaten within an inch of her life, her leg broken in three places, and a pretty awful infection setting in, but her power was formidable. She nearly took my head off with a spell, and would have, too, if Bastian hadn't thrown up a shield.

I healed her as much as I was able, the scars of her coven betraying her ones that I couldn't touch. We reunited her with Poppy, the pair of them heading to Georgia as soon as they could catch a flight. I tried to tell her that my decree didn't encompass either of them, but Shiloh wouldn't have it.

"Your mother infiltrated my coven using my face, Darby. You killed her while she was wearing my face. Shiloh St. James is dead. The Knoxville coven is dead. Let's keep it that way, shall we?"

I couldn't fault the logic in that, nor how clean it made everything. I foresaw some hiccups, but for now, it would keep. Or at least I hoped it would.

.   .   .

The next few days were an exercise in heartbreak and restraint. It didn't matter how many dead people I'd been around, how many ghosts, I hadn't dealt with this side of the fence in quite some time and never in this capacity. My dad had been a prominent member of the community. He'd been loved. And people wanted to pay their last respects.

I just wanted to lay in bed and cry. Or kill someone. That sounded good, too.

One thing I could say about it all was that Azrael had been right. I wasn't alone. J, Jimmy, Bishop, Sarina, and Sloane were on me like glue. Hell, my house was bursting with people either fixing food or giving hugs or asking how they could help, and I just wanted it all to stop. Everyone I'd ever met in my entire life brought by a casserole or a lasagna or a basket of muffins. I had more casserole dishes than I knew what to do with. Hell, even Mrs. Cooper brought by her famous fried chicken, but I just couldn't eat any of it.

J and Bishop had the good sense to kick everyone out for a few hours so I could mourn in peace, but even that didn't make me feel better.

I doubted anything would.

The day of the funeral was the fucking worst.

Because not only did I have to put on a dress and heels and watch my dad get put in the ground, but I also had to listen to everyone's kind words and get hugs from complete strangers while they told me the most asinine things. If one more person said he was in a better place now, or they were praying for me, or asked if I needed anything, I was going to scream.

At the end of the service, we went to the cemetery for the burial. The minister droned on about a plan for everything or some other such bullshit, like he hadn't just given a service twenty fucking minutes ago. If that wasn't bad enough, I was forced to ignore the ghosts that seemed to be flocking to me in droves, the buzz of their souls like a knife in my brain.

I tuned them all out, staring straight ahead as I tried not to smash things.

Sloane must have been reading my face because she sidled up next to me and rested her head on my shoulder. "Nothing I say can ever make this better. It fucking sucks. And it'll suck for a while. But, you're my big sister, and you know..." She paused, squeezing me in a sideways hug as she stared at her feet. "Well, we've got each other. You've always got me to shout at, tell me to go fuck myself, cry, you know...the things big sisters do."

Leaning my head against hers, I felt myself *want* to

smile but couldn't. "I'll remember that. I'm glad we have each other. Glad I found you." But I couldn't say anymore, and I think she knew it.

With a nod, Sloane squeezed my shoulder and went back to Bastian.

When it came time to toss dirt onto the top of his coffin, I summarily lost it. I couldn't stay there one more second, so as soon as the dirt left my fingertips, I stalked off. I didn't know where I was going, just away.

I found myself on a stone bench, far away from the other mourners, unwilling to subject myself to the after-burial coffee and cake bullshit. Honestly, how did people do this? And why? To delay being alone? To put themselves through hell? Was it a sport or a show or what?

I hated every single minute of this mess, and I wanted it all to just stop.

A man's footsteps crunched in the grass, breaking me out of my pity party and drawing my gaze up.

Can it be considered a pity party if you're at a funeral?

He was tall with white-blond hair, a shade I'd only seen on two other people in my life. His face was smooth and unlined, with dark brows over violet eyes that seemed to almost glow. Dressed in a dark-gray suit, he fit in with the other mourners, but he most definitely was not.

I might not have seen his face, but I knew without a doubt who this was. I shot to my feet, ready to do, I had no idea what, when he held up his hands in surrender.

"I take it you know who I am," my brother muttered, a look of chagrin on his face. Chagrin. Like he had bad manners and not like he was a mass-murdering fuck stick who'd set this whole bullshit into motion.

"What name would you like? X? Essex? The Overseer? You have a lot of names, brother."

The man had the fucking audacity to chuckle. "That I do."

"Why are you here? Offense completely intended, but this isn't the time. You want to kill me, great. We'll set an appointment to duke it out later."

Essex rubbed a hand over his mouth, likely hiding a grin at my cheek. "I have a proposition for you."

"At my dad's funeral? Read the room, man." I probably should feel scared, but all I wanted to do was punch him in his stupid fucking face. I'd been searching and not finding this man for far too long, and I couldn't do a damn thing about it right then.

Fucking figures.

"Not to mention it was your partner in crime that put him in the ground. I would rather put my hand in a woodchipper than listen to a word you have to say." I pivoted on a foot, ready to stalk off to a place where no one could find me.

"Fine. Don't say I didn't warn you," he said in a singsong voice, like all of this was a joke.

I turned back, ready to let him have it—audience be damned—but he was gone. In the place where he once stood was a piece of cardstock. I refused to touch this one—since I valued my life—and he had a penchant for blood curses. But I did manage to make out the lazy scrawl.

Azrael lied to you. Killian isn't where you think he is.
Come find me when you're ready for the truth.
—Essex

The truth?
Out of this family?
Sure.

Darby's story will continue with
Dead Shift
Grave Talker Book Four

GRAVE WATCH

Soul Reader Book Three

Meeting long-lost siblings should be awesome, right?

Well, when you happen to be on the wrong side of the law and have every intention of staying there, having a cop for a sister isn't exactly ideal. And teaming up with said sister? Well, that is just the cherry on top of the craptastic pie that has been my life.

But when our brother decides to attack us head on, banding together is the least of our problems.

Because in our family? Being the hunter also means being the hunted.

-Preorder now on Amazon-
Coming September 28, 2021

DEAD SHIFT

Grave Talker Book Four

Detective Darby Adler is about to hand in her badge.
After inadvertently taking the mantle of Warden of
Knoxville, Darby has painted a huge target on her back.
With bridges burned and the ABI on her tail, she'll have
to decide between staying a small-town detective or
leaning into her new role.

It's not only her job on the line—it's her life.

Who says small towns are boring?

-Preorder now on Amazon-
Coming November 16, 2021

SPELLS AND SLIP-UPS

The Wrong Witch Book One

I suck at witchcraft.

Coming from a long line of famous witches, I should be at the top of the heap. Problem is, if there is a spell cast anywhere in my vicinity, I will somehow mess it up. As a probationary agent with the Arcane Bureau of Investigation, I have two choices: I can limp along and *maybe* pass myself off as a competent agent, or I can fail. *Miserably.*

Worse news? If I can't get my act together, I may not only be out of a job, I could also lose my life.

Whose idea was this again?

Preorder now!
Coming June 7, 2022

THE ROGUE ETHEREAL SERIES

an adult urban fantasy series by Annie Anderson

Enjoy the Grave Talker Series?
Then you'll love Max!

Come meet Max. She's brash. She's inked. She has a bad habit of dying... *a lot*. She's also a Rogue with a demon on her tail and not much backup.
This witch has a serious bone to pick.

Check out the Rogue Ethereal Series today!

JOIN THE LEGION

EXCLUSIVE SNEAK PEEKS,
GIVEAWAYS, BOOK DISCUSSION.
COME FOR THE BOOKS.
STAY FOR THE MEMES.

To stay up to date on all things Annie Anderson, get exclusive access to ARCs and giveaways, and be a member of a fun, positive, drama-free space, join The Legion!

ABOUT THE AUTHOR

 Annie Anderson is the author of the international bestselling Rogue Ethereal series. A United States Air Force veteran, Annie pens fast-paced Urban Fantasy novels filled with strong, snarky heroines and a boatload of magic. When she takes a break from writing, she can be found binge-watching The Magicians, flirting with her husband, wrangling children, or bribing her cantankerous dogs to go on a walk.

To find out more about Annie and her books, visit www.annieande.com

Made in the USA
Las Vegas, NV
26 November 2021

35323335R00163